UNEXPECTED LOVE

L.S. PULLEN

Copyright © 2022 by L.S. Pullen

Unexpected Love

Text copyright © 2022 L.S. Pullen

All Rights Reserved

Published by: L.S. Pullen

Edited by: Liji Editing

Proofread by: Crystal Blanton

Cover Design & Formatting by: Leila Pullen

Photo: Licensed Stock

The right of L.S. Pullen to be identified as the author of the work has been asserted by her in accordance with the copyright, Designs and patents act 1988.

No part of this book may be reproduced in any form or by any electronic or mechanical means, including information storage and retrieval systems, without written permission from the author, except for the use of brief quotations in a book review.

All characters in this publication are fictional and any resemblance to real persons, living or dead is purely coincidental.

Dedication

To those of you who took a chance on my lockdown series, thank you xoxo

Author's Note

Due to adult content all my books are recommended for readers 18 years and over.

For detailed CW/TW please visit my Website

https://lspullen.co.uk/content-trigger-warnings

Thank you, and happy reading!

Quote

Because true love is always worth the wait.

Chapter One

Verity

I let out a cross between a growl and a groan, burying my face into my pillow to muffle my scream at being woken up for the third consecutive night by my arsehole baby brother—and when I say baby I use that term lightly, because Callum is a twenty-five-year-old man child.

If it wasn't for the sale of my house, I wouldn't currently be back in my childhood home. Rolling onto my back, I stare at my ceiling, which is covered in faded glow-in-the-dark stars, decorated by my said brother years ago—to be fair, they are pretty.

Just as my eyes begin to drift closed again, I hear Callum whisper-shout about being quiet.

If only he would take his own advice. There's a loud thud followed by a crash, and I know I need to go check he isn't vandalising our parents' house. They're away on a cruise he got them as an anniversary present, and even I must admit it was damn sweet of him.

But if my mum comes back to broken furniture, she won't go easy on him. It's about time he moved into a place of his own. I keep telling him, but he ignores me, for the most part.

There's another crash, and this time, I reach over and

switch on the lamp and toss the cover off me and throw my legs over the edge of the bed. I make my way over to my bedroom door, which is still adorned with a One Direction boyband poster.

I open my door quietly in case he's out in the hallway with someone—it wouldn't be the first time I've caught him with his hand up someone's skirt or his tongue down someone's throat. Granted, he tends to only bring people back when my parents aren't here, but still, it's not something any sister needs to bear witness to.

Creeping out into the hallway, the floorboards creak from years of use from a family of six. Other than the house I recently left, this is the only other home I've ever known.

As I approach Callum's door, I notice it's ajar and hold my breath as I take a quick peek inside. I exhale when I see he's collapsed horizontally at the foot of his bed. He's still in his jeans, thank goodness, but only has one shoe on. I creep in to remove it before retreating, closing his door shut with a soft click before going to the bathroom.

Just as I'm about to head back to bed, I hear voices coming from downstairs and let out a frustrated groan.

"What the fuck?"

Please don't tell me he's left random strangers in our mum's living room.

Resigning myself to the fact I need to go and check, I make my way downstairs but skip the stairs that make the most noise, not wanting to alert anyone to my presence.

I'm just rounding the banister at the bottom of the stairs when I see the TV is on and let out a sigh of relief as I make a move to switch it off.

But I freeze when I see the large silhouette of a person. Taking another quiet step forward, I let out a silent breath as I get a side profile view of Callum's best friend, Liam. The colours from the television wash over him in a dim glow. The sound of a woman panting draws my attention to the TV screen and what's actually playing —porn.

Just as I'm about to storm over and switch it off, the sound of a deep moan emanates from Liam, causing me to pause. My eyes trail down south, coming to a stop when I see his hand wrapped around his cock, his head tilted back, his eyes closed, and his tongue digging into the inside of his cheek.

I swallow hard. Fucking hell.

Liam has always been a good-looking guy, and even when he was younger there was no denying it, but since he turned eighteen, I swear it's impossible not see how ruggedly handsome he is. Tall, dark hair, blue eyes, and don't even get me started on those abs you could ping a pound coin off.

I am aware I shouldn't even have these thoughts. He's over five years younger than me, but I'm only human.

Besides, there is seriously something hot about watching a man touching his shaft like that—the way he works his wrist and twists his hand over the head.

I feel my lower region begin to tingle as I continue to watch him, my nipples harden beneath the too tight nightshirt I'm wearing, and my entire body begins to heat.

My eyes roam back to the TV at the sounds of heavy grunting and panting. There's a side view of a woman on all fours, peering over her shoulder as a man the size of Goliath has her hair in his grasp as he fucks her senseless.

Where does someone even find this shit? That accompanied by the soft grunts from Liam draws my focus back to him, and hell if my breathing doesn't start to increase. This whole scenario is turning me the fuck on.

I should just turn around and go back to bed, but my brain and my body aren't fucking co-operating.

I swallow, biting down on my lower lip. It's been a while since I've had any action that wasn't with my battery-operated friend. Well, over a year to be exact, after I finally got the courage to end my relationship of eight years, because James just wasn't right for me. Don't get me wrong, on paper he was, but in reality not so much. Probably didn't help that he had a habit of dipping his wick in other candles, if you will.

My hand trembles, moving of its own accord, slipping under the waistband of my sleep shorts and to the apex of my thighs, and I'm not surprised to find I'm wet.

I came down expecting to kick some randoms out, but instead, I catch Liam wanking off to a porno.

The louder he gets the more turned on I become, and then before I can think better of it or come to my senses, my finger slips between my folds, causing me to reposition my feet. The floor beneath me creaks loudly and Liam's head turns in my direction.

He turns to face me fully, his head tilted to the side, but he doesn't even seem surprised. Unable to stop myself, my eyes travel down again to his open jeans and his dick, which is like a steel rod in his grip. Fuck me, he's hung like a horse.

His gaze flickers down to where my hand is buried inside my shorts and I quickly pull it free, embarrassed from not only being caught watching him but also touching myself in the process.

Chapter Two

Liam

Surely, it's my drunk state and the vision before is an apparition? There's no other plausible explanation as to why standing before me is my deepest desire and hottest wet dream come true. I blink and then glance down as Verity quickly pulls her hand free of her shorts, her cheeks scarlet, and her lips parted in utter shock.

She's always been gorgeous but standing before me in only a white button-down nightshirt and those tiny bed shorts leaving her long legs bare is like a hit of adrenaline.

Even with her dark hair in a messy side knot and those pretty brown eyes so dark in this muted light, I'm completely entranced.

I squeeze myself hard once before letting go and moving towards her, keeping my steps slow, expecting her to disappear at any moment. And when she doesn't, I reach out my hand, needing to see if she's real or just a figment of my imagination. My thumb swipes over her velvet soft lips, the ones I've dreamt about more than I care to admit.

A soft gasp escapes her and my dick twitches as her hot breath blows across the pad of my thumb.

I move my hand to the back of her neck and squeeze,

drawing her closer. She looks up at me with wide eyes, and everything in my inebriated brain is trying to tell me to stop. I've only ever let myself go with her one other time, and it's not like she knew it was me.

Just this once, I want to ignore my sensible side.

Why can't I be reckless for a change?

Because it's Verity.

I squeeze my eyes closed. Her scent is powerful, and not in an overpowering way but in an intoxicating way. If she was in the same vicinity as me, I would always be able to find her by her sweet fragrance alone.

This must be a dream, she can't be here, and then Callum's words start to come back in blurry waves… Verity is staying here until the sale of her house. She split up with her partner, and about fucking time too.

He was never good enough for her. No one will ever be good enough for her.

Opening my eyes, hers are watching me, as if she's still caught under a spell and at any moment it could break.

"Are you drunk?" she whispers, as if coming back to reality.

I nod and raise my other hand, my thumb and forefinger barely touching.

"A little."

She lets out a soft laugh and shakes her head, and when I glance down towards her chest, my breath catches when I see the flash of silver. I reach out for it, my thumb and forefinger brushing over the silver locket which is warm to the touch from being pressed against her skin.

It gives me a strange sense of satisfaction that she still wears it, even though she never knew it was from me.

Inscribed on the front is 'Cariad', meaning love, beloved or sweetheart, and when opened it has two heart shape spaces and a rare Welsh gold heart charm above the locket.

She looks down at my thumb stroking the heart shape.

"I can't believe you still wear this," I say, my voice almost a whisper.

Shit, I hadn't intended to say it out loud. My eyes follow the hollow of her throat when she swallows.

"What? It was from you?"

I saved a year's worth of my paper round money to get it for her eighteenth birthday. She'd lost the one her grandad had given her whilst we were at the beach the year before, and then he passed away shortly after. She was devastated, so I started saving.

Her eyes spring to mine and her lips part, but no words come out.

"It hurt me to see you so sad after you lost the locket from your grandad."

"I didn't know," she whispers.

I clear my throat, because I had never planned on telling her, and now she knows.

The haze I'm caught in dissipates as the sound of footsteps start to sluggishly descend the stairs and I glance down at myself, standing with my hard-on between us, my hand still on the back of her neck, holding her in place. Fuck.

I'm not too drunk to know this is going to be a cluster fuck if Callum finds us like this.

My adrenaline spikes as my heartbeat races, and in one swift movement, I step forward and push her back towards the alcove of the stairs.

She looks confused and opens her mouth to say something, but I quickly cover her mouth with my hand and a muffled sound vibrates against my palm along with her soft breath which tickles.

I know the moment she realises that Callum is about to round the banister as her eyes go wide, and I lean into her until I'm flush against her, my erection resting against her lower stomach. Even with the material of her nightshirt between us, I can feel her warmth, causing my dick to twitch. Her eyes go wide as I suck in a hiss through my teeth.

I reach down and squeeze my base in an attempt to try and calm myself, and to try and tuck it back into my jeans, but when I feel her tongue touch the palm of my hand still covering her mouth, I freeze.

Callum is behind us now. I can hear him stumbling about towards the kitchen. I watch as Verity's eyes track his movements, her chest rising and falling.

A cupboard door crashes open, and I cringe—it wouldn't be the first time he's accidentally pulled one off in a drunken state.

But this… being this close to Verity is really fucking dangerous.

Having my body pressed up against hers like this is a test of wills, and when she shifts on her feet, I glance down as she squeezes her thighs together. I breathe her in and let out a deep groan as I lean closer. Her eyelids flutter closed as I bring my lips to the shell of her ear and whisper, "You know I can smell how turned on you are, Verity. I can feel how hard your nipples are through the fabric of your nightshirt."

It's something I wouldn't say in my right mind but fuck it.

She muffles a response under my hand and I lower it, expecting her to push me away and tell me how disgusting I am, but instead, she shocks the hell out of me when she swallows loudly before whispering her own response.

"I can't help it."

Fucking hell, I need to take a step back, physically and emotionally.

Being this close to her is dangerous and it's short circuiting my damn brain.

"Careful, V," I say louder, with an edge of warning to my voice.

But when she bites down on her lower lip, the frayed thread I was clinging to fucking snaps. And then I do something that even surprises the hell out of me. I lower my hand to her outer thigh and squeeze. The pitch of her breathing increases and her eyes are trained on mine. I don't want to blink. I don't want to risk missing anything as she looks at me with something akin to lust.

Moving my hand to her rear, I push up and under her shorts and cup her bare arse cheek, causing her to arch into me with a soft moan.

Shit!

In the distance, Callum is still bashing around in the kitchen, but in this moment, I'm a slave to Verity.

"V, you need to go back upstairs," I say through clenched teeth. My touch is the complete opposite to my words, as my fingers trail over the velvety soft skin of her arse cheek and back around to the front of her shorts, sliding up to the apex between her legs. When they make contact with her wet folds, I think I've died and gone to heaven.

I am well and truly fucked.

Chapter Three

Verity

What the actual fuck is even happening right now?

Liam is pressed against me, his fingers teasing me as he slides them through my folds. My head bumps against the wall as I throw my head back and groan at the contact, because damn it feels so good to be touched. His other hand leaves the back of my neck and holds onto my hip.

Right before he slides in his finger, hooking it inside me, my channel squeezes and pulses, and my eyes spring open and meet his—they're full of lust, want, and desire.

"Oh fuck," I hiss under my breath as he moves it in an expert manner before he adds another and moves them both in a 'come here' motion as my inner walls grope him.

Right as I forget where I am or what I'm doing, my brother comes stumbling back into the living room, and for a brief moment, I think we've been caught; it isn't until he throws his head back and laughs, I realise he's facing the television and not us.

I let out a breath. The thought of being caught is both exhilarating and terrifying in equal measures.

And then, before my brain can catch up, Liam lowers his mouth to mine, his lips pressing against mine softly in a silent question, and a small gasp escapes me as he gains access.

His tongue sweeping inside of my mouth matches the movement of his fingers.

Oh. My. God.

I squeeze my eyes shut. The sound of Callum's footsteps are heavy overhead as he goes back upstairs.

Lost in the kiss, it takes me a few seconds before I freeze, because this is familiar, and even though it only happened the once, I'd know these lips anywhere.

Fuck.

Liam tenses and pulls his face back, his eyes boring into mine.

"It was *you*," I say on an exhale.

He nods his head once, but his fingers continue to work me into a state of ecstasy. I lose focus when he lowers his mouth back to mine, and I undulate my hips, desperate for more friction between us, the heel of his hand pressing against my clit.

I feel his other hand as he moves it up and over my chest. I think he's going to touch my breasts, but he keeps going, palming the back of my neck again, only this time, he presses the pad of his thumb to the hollow of my throat.

A guttural moan escapes me—I'm so caught up in the euphoria of the moment.

Up until now my arms have been hanging either side of me like extra limbs, and coming to my senses, I move to take hold of his hot, hard shaft—the way the veins are so prominent, his skin soft like cashmere.

Liam thrusts into my touch, his lips leaving mine as he hisses out a curse.

"Fuck, V."

I know I shouldn't be here, not with him and not like this, but I don't think I have ever wanted something with such desperation before. I'm wound up, coiled so tight as he expertly fucks me fast with his fingers, and I go onto my tiptoes and grind down on his hand.

My knuckles tighten around him, silently urging him, begging him to go harder, faster. I love how he doesn't need any more coaxing as he does just what I need and matches my vigour, giving me exactly what I crave.

"Ahh, yes, shit, Liam."

His forehead rests against mine now, our heavy breaths mingling as he fucks my hand and I fuck his fingers.

The sound of the porno playing in the background only amplifies the erotic chorus of sounds coming from us.

"Do you want to stop?" he grunts out.

I shake my head. "No." I don't miss the fact he never said we *should* stop, only did *I* want to stop.

He pulls back slightly. "Thank fuck for that," he says, giving me the most mesmerising smile I think I've ever seen, and then his mouth crashes down on mine.

This time, he devours me with his kiss, but it's more like he's staking his claim, it's a silent exchange that something profound has changed between us and there's no going back, and in this moment, I am completely at his mercy.

My pleasure builds, cresting, and I know I won't last much longer—and from the way his dick has grown even harder, it would appear neither will he.

But this is not a race to the finish line, it's as though we both want to draw this out, savour every second for as long as humanly possible.

So, when his fingers slip free from me with a wet sound, I can't help the mewling sound that escapes me, and my eyes spring open.

But before I even have a chance to moan or protest about the loss, he drops to his knees, his intention clear as he drags my shorts down my thighs and legs, holding each foot up for me to step out of them, and then without any fan fair, he grips my leg behind the knee and hooks it over his shoulder.

I reach out to steady myself, my hand going to the crown of his head, my fingers gripping his hair.

The sound of him inhaling my arousal with a deep moan is all I hear before my pulse thumps loudly in my ears as he spreads me wide with his fingers, darting out his tongue and plunging it inside me as deep as he can go.

"Fucking hell," I whimper.

I look down, watching the way he savours my pussy like it's his last meal, and it's only now I notice his other hand has moved to his cock as he pumps his shaft in quick succession.

Hungry to come and hungry to touch him, I know I want it all.

"I need to touch you," I say on a breathy exhale, and his eyes roam up to meet mine.

He draws back gently, moving my leg off his shoulder until my foot joins the other one back on the floor. Standing to his full height, his beard glistens with my arousal, and I reach up to wipe his top lip. He turns into my touch, my palm against his cheek, and the moment feels intimate as the air grows thick around us.

He takes hold of the back of my wrist, leads me over to the sofa and lays down. He's well over six foot, but it's a four-seater so it just about accommodates his height. I just stand there when he looks at me and says, "Sit on my face, V."

I swallow and move towards him, but he shakes his head.

"No, facing the other way."

His eyes are dark, dangerous, he's forbidden, and yet, I can't even bring myself to care, not right now, not with the need and ache I feel deep between my thighs.

There's no graceful way to do this, so I end up stepping onto the edge of the sofa, my weight sinking into the plush leather padding as I straddle either side of him and then lower myself, my arse level with his face, and his cock level with mine.

Without giving me even a moment's grace, his hands tug on my hips and down to his face as I cover his mouth.

I groan from the contact, my forehead dipping forward, the masculine scent of his arousal filling my senses. His tongue sweeps from my back passage and through to my soaking wet folds.

Leaning on my elbow, I reach out for him. He's circumcised—I've never been with a guy without his foreskin before. But before I ponder the thought too much, I lower my face and bring his steel hard shaft towards my face. Flicking out my tongue, I circle over his large head, lapping up the pre-cum before taking him into my mouth. He's bigger than what I'm used to, and I feel him stiffen even more and know he's holding back from thrusting to the back of my throat.

He's fucking me senseless with his mouth, tongue, and fingers. I can barely hold myself upright as my weight bears down on his face, smothering him. But I don't think he cares as his hands go to my hips, pulling me down harder, his tongue spearing into my channel.

The television is still playing the soundtrack of the porno in the background, and I moan around his cock, saliva running down my chin as my eyes begin to water. I struggle for breath as I begin to crest, my climax slamming into me. I have to pull my mouth free from his dick as I spasm and come all over his face.

Chapter Four

Liam

Me in my right mind wouldn't be doing this—fucking Verity's pussy with my mouth—and yet, here I am, with the woman of my dreams detonating on my tongue and fingers.

I'm so close my balls tighten, and my dick has never felt so damn hard. She stopped sucking me off when her orgasm hit, and I'm glad—I love getting to savour her pleasure as it courses through her.

Her hand moves back to my dick, and it jumps at the contact. I thrust up, unable to stop myself, and she takes me back to her throat. I pull my face away from her wet pussy but keep my fingers where they are as her walls continue to clench around them relentlessly.

"Fuck, V. You need to stop or I'm coming in your mouth," I grunt out, trying to hold off, but it's impossible, I'm past the point of return and my orgasm explodes in hot, long bursts straight into her mouth and down her throat. She swallows every drop until I'm completely spent, but my thumb is working her clit, my fingers still pumping into her.

When she releases my now semi-hard dick, I can hear her erratic intake of breath as she moans.

"God."

I speed up my ministrations as she rides my fingers, giving me the perfect view of her cunt and her arse.

"Come again for me, V, show me what you've got."

And just like that, she goes rigid, her walls clamping around my fingers as she convulses and comes, her channel thick and hot. She rides it out until she collapses on top of my thighs, breathless.

Removing my fingers, I bring them to my face and lick them. Never has anyone tasted as fucking divine as Verity Warren.

Leaning forward, I bite down on her arse cheek and tap her thigh, coaxing her to move. She sluggishly lifts herself up, and I pull her back against my chest. She stretches out her legs and I adjust us so we're spooning.

We're both breathing heavy, neither of us saying anything. Maybe we're both too stunned to speak? But I just want to savour this moment for as long as I can before the reality of the situation catches up with us.

I blink awake having dosed off, which is weird for me as I've been struggling to sleep at night recently. I look over to the TV which has shut itself off, so I must have been asleep for a good few hours at least.

Verity is still pressed against me, her breathing deep, and I know she's sleeping. As carefully as I can, I manage to get out from behind her without jostling her too much, and then when I'm sure she's still sound asleep, I reach down and pull her into my arms. My dick rubs uncomfortably against the crotch of my jeans, but I ignore it until I'm upstairs and softly lowering her onto the bed.

"Because flamingos are pretty," she mumbles, and I can't help but smile.

Pulling the cover up and over her, I smooth her hair away from her face as it surrounds her in soft, dark halo waves. And then I allow myself to watch her for a few blissful minutes, because come tomorrow, I'll go back to keeping her at arm's length, because she's still not attainable. To her, I'm just her kid brother's best friend, but to me, she'll always be so much more.

But I'll save us the awkwardness of her telling me she was caught up in the moment, and I'll act as if this has never happened, even though it's now branded to the recess of my soul.

Leaning over, I switch off the lamp, and once my eyes adjust, I look up to the ceiling and smile. Callum said I was an idiot for doing that, covering her ceiling in glow-in-the-dark stars, but he let me do it anyway. She presumed it was him, of course, and he didn't bother to correct her—he was an accomplice, after all.

Bending down, I kiss her softly on the forehead and give her one last look before I retreat, closing her door behind me.

I make use of the bathroom while I'm up here and then check on Callum. He's snoring, his jeans now at his ankles, and I can't help but laugh as I go in and pull them off over his feet and lift his legs onto the mattress and leave him to sleep.

It was his idea to go out tonight, seeing as he's going to Devon to work on his manuscript for a couple of weeks, and I only came back into town yesterday after spending a fortnight with my parents in Kent, but I miss being here and near the city. You can take the boy out of Camden, but not Camden out of the boy.

Of course, I had every intention of booking into an Airbnb, but he gave me shit and told me to have his room, said he'd already cleared it with his mum and dad, Linda and Barry, and said it would look rude if I didn't.

Honestly, I'm still surprised he hasn't moved out yet. As much as I love my parents, as soon as I was eighteen and saved enough for a deposit, I was out of there and got myself a house share. And then at twenty, I signed up to the Army and became a combat medical technician.

I knew pretty much early on I wouldn't stay past my fourth year, so I gave my notice a year ago and now here I am in limbo.

Honestly, I'm not sure what I'll do. I knew it was going to be hard being in the armed forces, but nothing really prepares you for it.

It's taking some getting used to, transitioning back into civilian life—I didn't quite comprehend how much until now. I don't know what my aspirations are or what I want to do as my future career but I'm going to take a beat, and hopefully, I'll work it out sooner rather than later.

But what just happened with Verity was completely unexpected, and I savoured every moment of it.

I splash my face with cold water and stare at my reflection. Callum's always been good at keeping me up to date with life outside of the army, and I won't lie about the fact that when he told me Verity had finally broken up with the knob head she'd been living with, I felt lighter somehow.

When I kissed her and she froze, I knew the moment recognition hit—I've only kissed her one other time, back when I was eighteen. It was at her twenty third masquerade party. And the arsehole who she evidently ended up moving in with had just cheated on her, *again*.

The memory is so vivid. I was outside, about to smoke a sneaky joint, when she came out. She was on her own, and what I noticed straight away was that she was crying. And honestly, if it hadn't been for those tears, I might have stayed hidden in the shadows.

I'd stepped into the light, enough for her to see me, and I could tell she was a bit tipsy. The thought of leaving her alone outside did not sit well with me.

Walking over, I handed her a handkerchief from my suit pocket. Callum and I didn't mess about, we went all in with our attire. He had his eye on one of her friends who he was currently fucking in the disabled toilet of the hall her parents had hired out.

She'd thanked me and pulled out a tiny mirror from her clutch and cleaned up her tears as best she could, and it was only when she started talking that I realised she had no idea it was me.

It was nice. I felt like I didn't have to hide behind how I felt about her, like I usually did.

"You don't say much, do you?"

I laugh and shrug my shoulders and touch my mask, making sure it's still in place. It's been nice listening to her rambling on to be honest.

"Well, thank you for the handkerchief," she says, waving it at me and stuffing it into her small clutch.

"Hey, is that a joint?" She points to my top pocket, and I run my fingers through my hair. Shit, I forgot I put it there.

I nod and she wiggles her fingers for me to hand it over, so I do, and then she holds out her other hand.

"Lighter," she says quietly.

"Oh." I pull it out of my pocket and hand it to her. It's not one of those throw away ones, it's one I got from Camden market last time Callum and I were out.

She sparks up the spliff and takes a long shallow drag and then holds the joint out for me, but just as I'm about to take it, she moves her hand away and goes up on tip toes, her mouth inches from mine. And I can't hide my smile as she makes her intentions clear. I part my lips as she blows it back into my mouth. I inhale long and deep and then exhale, getting a light buzz.

But it's what she does next that completely renders me at her mercy when her lips crash over my mouth, her tongue seeking access, which I happily oblige before I push her back against the wall, my hands moving to her face as I take control of the kiss.

. . .

Up until tonight, that was one of the best nights of my life. We made out for a good ten minutes before one of her drunk friends came barrelling out in search of her. I slipped back into the shadows as her friend dragged her back inside to the party, and I never did get my lighter back.

Chapter Five

Verity

I wake up feeling rested, better than I have in a long time, but also in desperate need to relieve myself. While I'm sitting there, it all comes flooding back to me, and I cover my face with my hand.

"Shit, shit, shit."

Not only did I make out with Liam last night, but I also gave him head while he fucked me with his mouth and gave me the most intense orgasm—no, plural orgasms—I've ever experienced.

And the revelation—no, revelations—that not only was my locket from him but *he* was also the mystery gift giver. But even more surprising is he was the guy I kissed at my masquerade party. All this time I thought it was a random stranger, but no, it was my little brother's best friend.

"Fuck."

The irony was I never intended on kissing him, but he had such delicious looking lips, and he gave me a damn hankey. I was upset and angry over James—God, even back then there were red flags. So, I took what I wanted in the moment and stole a kiss from the man in the mask. Which was also my way of saying 'up yours' to James. But that kiss was something else… I didn't want it to end. I wanted so much more. If it hadn't have been for my friend, Ali, coming to find me, who the hell knows what would have happened?

But all this time it was Liam, and I never fucking knew.

I still can't get over the way he looked at me last night when I caught him. Anyone would have expected him to be embarrassed, but he just looked as though I was some kind of magical being. But it's more than that, he's always had a way of seeing through the facade I put on for everyone else, and that's bloody un-nerving. But last night was out of this world, even if he was drunk.

Oh my God, I took advantage of him while he was drunk.

Washing my hands and then brushing my teeth, I contemplate going back to my room to hide like the coward I am, but it's happened now.

What would Ali say? "Own your truths, girl."

Going back to my room, I pull on a pair of joggers and then gingerly I make my way downstairs, tuning my head to the side as if it will improve my hearing and my chances of hearing if Liam is stirring. When I'm satisfied all is quiet, I descend the last stair and round the banister. I glance towards the alcove of the stairs and immediately my cheeks burn, and my lower stomach tightens.

Discarded on the floor are my sleep shorts, and I scurry over and quickly snatch them up. A noise catches my attention from the other side of the sofa, and I find myself tiptoeing until I round it.

Laying there, with an arm slung over his face, is indeed Liam. He has a blanket pulled up to his hips, just where his hand dips, resting on his groin. He's so damn handsome. Sometimes it hurts to look at him for too long.

Callum could have got the blow-up bed if he wasn't so wasted. My brother's old rooms are both a mess as they're in the middle of having them decorated, which means everything is crammed into one while the other is being done. But at least he has a blanket this time—my dad once found him sleeping on the sofa under a cushion.

And then I'm hit with the vivid memory of his cock in my mouth as it flashes through my mind, and again, my body tingles to life. The way he smelt, the way he tasted like my every deepest desire… just everything about him is so fucking masculine, with those hard lines and his soft touch. He exudes pure, unadulterated heat. My only annoyance is he was clothed—it would have been nice to have seen him in all his naked splendour.

Shit. Caught in a lust filled haze, I blink away my wondering thoughts and clear my throat, before turning on my heels and heading into the kitchen. I need some caffeine to get my head around the repercussions of what happened with the two of us last night.

I make myself a cup of tea and head into my parents' conservatory. It gets the best light in here during the morning and I love watching the birds as they use the water bath and the bird feeders my mum has dotted around the garden.

Sitting on one of the soft chairs, I tuck my legs underneath me and hug my mug. Tilting my face up towards the skylight above, rainbows of sunlight dance in front of my eyelids, the warmth seeping into my skin.

Finishing my tea, I check my watch and take a deep breath. I need to go get ready for work. To be honest, there's nothing wrong with my job, it's just monotonous—working in accounting wasn't anything I ever really wanted to do.

It's why I envy Callum. I love how he pursued his passion with his writing, and I wish I had the confidence to do that.

Maybe it's why I haven't told anyone, not even my closest friends that I started a small business on the side—vinyl designs, T-shirts, tote bags… loads of stuff really. I always wanted to put my graphic designs to use, and I when I couldn't find something I wanted, I decided to just create it myself, and here I am almost six months later.

Granted, it was easier after James moved out, thank God. There is no way I could have stayed living with him after our breakup.

But now, with all my belongings in storage while I try and find somewhere else to live, my printer and cutting machine and materials are all crammed into my childhood room. If my dad was curious, he never asked. It's what I like about him—he doesn't push, he waits until you're ready. He's always been such a patient man.

My mum, on the other hand wouldn't be so generous, but luckily for me, she was too busy getting ready for their cruise to pay me and my belongings too much mind.

I slide the conservatory door shut and then turn around, walking straight into a rock-hard chest.

"Shit, sorry."

Before I even glance up, I already know it's Liam from his scent and the distinct rumble of his laughter.

Swallowing hard, I try to step back, but I'm met with the glass of the door.

"You okay there, V?" Liam asks, catching my empty mug before it hits the floor.

I nod and clear my throat; he's staring at me, and I squirm under his gaze.

"What?" I all but hiss and feel like an absolute bitch.

He shakes his head and moves aside for me to pass, holding his hands up, my mug hanging off his middle and index fingers.

"Nothing, you just looked deep in thought, and I was just coming to check on you," he says, his voice deep, inviting, and sexy… fuck. Did I find it sexy before last night? Goosebumps erupt all over my body, my nipples go taut against the fabric of my nightshirt, and my stomach flutters with excitement.

And I know the moment he notices—the way his eyes trail down my body, his head slightly tilted. I shake my head to clear the fog.

"I'm going to be late for work," I say, my voice coming out scratchy as I brush past him.

His low chuckle follows me all the way out of the kitchen and up the stairs, where I run into another hard chest, only this time, it's Callum.

"Slow your horses," he says, steadying me.

I step back and clip him around the earhole. "Ouch, what was that for?" He groans.

"Oh please, it was a butterfly kiss, and that was for waking me up, *again*."

He winces and at least as the good grace to look a little contrite.

"Sorry, V, I wanted to hit the town with Liam. I go away today, and he only got back into town yesterday."

At his mention of Liam, I feel my cheeks begin to heat and I have to look away.

"Well, at least I get the place to myself while you're in Devon." I miss having my own space. It's funny how once James moved out, I noticed how much I like my own company. Or mostly didn't like his... who knows?

Callum laughs and shakes his head. "No, Liam's staying, I already cleared it with Mum and Dad, not that I needed to, I still pay them rent whether I'm here or not."

I cross my arms. "Oi, I intend to pay towards being here," I say, and then his words catch up with me. "Wait... what? Liam is staying here? For how long?"

Callum shrugs and lets out a wide yawn as he answers, "A few weeks."

I cover my nose with my hand. "You smell like a brewery, make sure you eat a loaded breakfast and hold off on driving up until later, you smell like you're still over the limit."

He rubs his temple and gives me a boyish grin. "Yes, Mum, will do."

Flipping him off, he laughs at my retreating back as I try not to freak out about living under the same roof as Liam, alone for the next couple of weeks.

Chapter Six

Liam

I pretended to be asleep when I heard Verity come downstairs this morning, and I knew it was her from the sound of her footsteps—Callum is anything but quiet, but with her there's always been a graceful way she carries herself, almost like she carries herself on the tips of her toes rather than on the heels of her feet. I'm not even sure she's aware of doing it, but I am—I notice everything about Verity.

A big part of me thinks it will be best if I just book the Airbnb, but then Callum will ask questions and I don't want to openly lie to him. I mean, yes, I could wait until he's in Devon, but he'll know something's up.

With my arm over my face, I listened to Verity as she made herself a cup of tea, and then there was the slide of the conservatory door opening and closing and I knew she'd gone to sit in there. She reminds me of a cat looking for a hot spot.

I expected her to maybe be out there for ten minutes at most, but after twenty, my curiosity got the better of me when she didn't come back inside.

Standing on the other side of the door, I watched her through the glass. Her eyes were closed but I could see them moving behind the lids of her eyes, and I guess that maybe I was worried she was freaking out about what we got up to, but from her body language, she seemed quite relaxed. For a split second, I allowed my mind to go back to what happened with us last night. I try not to get my hopes up, but for me, it was a long time coming. But for her, I have no doubt it was all a shock.

So, yeah, I'll keep standing on the side-lines, hoping like hell it won't be awkward between us, even now I've had more of a taste, because kissing her when I was eighteen in contrast to kissing her seven years later is a whole different experience entirely.

Caught up in my own thoughts, I was too late to back away when she came back into the kitchen. I didn't even see her get up, I was too consumed with thoughts of my tongue feasting on her sweet as sin pussy.

She looked equal parts pissed and aroused when she bumped into me, not that I was complaining—having her so close will never get old, not for me.

I couldn't help but chuckle as she made a hasty getaway and quickly disappeared back upstairs. I heard Callum's muffled voice as he was no doubt talking to her, as I made myself a tea and him a strong coffee, because as intoxicated as I might have been, he was way worse.

"Hey, man," he says when he comes out to join me, as I sit in the chair Verity vacated.

"You look like shit," I say as he drops down into a chair opposite.

He just shrugs. "Well, it was worth it, we haven't been out like that in ages."

I smile. "Yeah, it was a great night," I admit, but probably not for the same reason he might think.

"I'm not going to be leaving until later this afternoon. Verity might have had a point about my blood alcohol levels." He scrubs his hand over his face. "So, if you want to swing by the hotel later, we can grab your stuff before I hit the road."

Contemplating his question, I just nod. It's not like I have a mode of transport at the minute because I sold my car when I went into the army, and to be fair, I don't really mind jumping on the tube or bus, not when I'm so close to the city.

"Hey, can you do me a favour?"

I glance back over to Callum, who now has a serious look on his face.

"Can you keep an eye on Verity? I know she's my big sister, but I still worry about her. She just seems more withdrawn lately." He shrugs. "Hell, I don't know, maybe it's more noticeable since she's staying here."

Swallowing down the lump in my throat, I force myself to ask the question, "Do you think it's because of her breakup with the dick, Jimbo? Like, maybe she's not over him or something?" I can't bear to say his actual name—James—out loud, it just leaves a sour taste in my mouth.

He turns to look at me and shakes his head. "Honestly, your guess is as good as mine. They've not been together for almost a year, but then again, what the hell do I know about love?"

I smile at the thought. She's over her ex, one less thing to worry over, but I also can't help but laugh when I reply, "Enough to write best-selling romance novels, apparently." I raise my brow.

He throws his head back and laughs at that. "And I'll be fucked if I know how that happened. I swear I get a serious case of imposter syndrome at least once a day."

"Well don't, man. I, for one, am proud of you."

His cheeks heat from my praise. "Mate, I'm way too hungover for all this soppy shit. Come on, fancy a walk to the cafe with me, get a big arse fry up?"

I nod and push to my feet. "Yeah, but I need to shower first. You got something I can change into?"

The thought of washing remnants of Verity from my skin pains me, but the thought of sitting next to my best mate without washing makes me feel like an arsehole too.

"Yeah, course."

Letting out a groan, he pushes to his feet and follows me back into the kitchen, and we put our mugs in the dishwasher.

"Since when did I go from being able to function after a night out to feeling like I've been run over by a damn freight train?" Callum asks with a whiny voice.

"Because you're old," Verity says, walking into the kitchen with her head cast down as she rummages through her bag.

My breath gets caught in my throat—she's a vision. Her dark hair is pulled back in a low bun at the nape of her neck and images of me freeing it and wrapping it around my fist slam into me. I shake the thought away as I gaze down the length of her body. She's in a skirt suit that hugs every single fucking delectable curve, her legs are bare, and she has on a pair of black stilettos. If she was wearing glasses too, I swear I'd have to leave the room.

She glances up and her cheeks tinge pink when she makes eye contact with me. I have to stifle my moan when I spot the deep red lipstick she's wearing, making her hazel eyes pop.

Fuck my life.

"Says you," he retorts. "You're practically an old age pensioner yourself."

Pulling her hand free from her bag, she flips him. "Ha bloody ha. I'm only five years older than you, moron."

He raises his eyebrows and looks at me. "Oh, you see that, Liam? Now it's only five years, like its nothing, no big deal. I recall you being embarrassed to be seen with us when we were eighteen."

She visibly swallows, because now she knows it was indeed me that she kissed when I was eighteen, and her cheeks bloom red. I watch the hollow of her throat move from the action as vivid memories from last night come back with full force. It takes everything in me not to adjust myself, or worse, walk up to her and kiss that lipstick right off her lips.

Chapter Seven

Verity

The way his blue eyes grow dark and almost stormy, it's not hard to imagine where his thoughts are going because mine are probably right there alongside his as my brother's comment slams into me, and I suddenly feel like such a hypocrite.

"I wasn't that bad," I reply quietly and make my way towards the fridge, sucking in a breath as I pass Liam. His lip curves just a fraction, but I try not to draw any more attention to myself as I go to retrieve my lunch.

Pulling the door open, I look for my pasta that I made last night, but it's missing.

"Callum, please don't tell me you ate my lunch."

His head appears around the side of the door. "What was your lunch?" he asks.

I raise an eyebrow. "Tuna pasta, it was in a small Tupperware container. I left it right there," I say, pointing to the empty space on the shelf.

Giving me a toothy grin, his eyes go wide. "If you mean the empty Tupperware container that's in my room, that would be yes."

Closing my eyes, I take a deep breath and let out a sigh.

"Wonderful," I say and slam the fridge door closed with maybe more force than necessary.

"I'm sorry, V, I was hungry last night and needed to soak up the alcohol. And honestly, I was too drunk to consider it wasn't fair game."

I glance to Liam who looks away—he's probably thinking what I am, that's right, we were making out in the alcove of the stairs while he was raiding the fridge, completely unaware.

"It's fine. I just have a meeting at lunchtime, so I won't be able to grab anything."

Reaching out, I open the cupboard and search for a granola bar, and then grab an apple and banana from the fruit bowl before dropping them into my bag.

Callum slings his arm over my shoulder. "I really am sorry," he says, sounding like a child all over again, before kissing the side of my temple.

"Callum, get off me, you stink."

And he does, he smells like a damp beer mat.

He sniffs under his armpit.

"Eww, you're disgusting," I say, laughing as I push him away.

"Thanks. Don't think I haven't noticed how I'm the only one you're giving shit to. Liam was just as drunk as I was."

I'm about to answer when Liam, who up until now hasn't said a word, speaks.

"No, I wasn't, Callum. I was drunk, whereas you, on the other hand were wasted. You couldn't even say the address when I hailed us down a taxi."

Callum just shrugs and I shake my head.

"Yeah, well, I knew I was safe with you," he says, fluttering his eyelids and putting his arm around Liam's shoulders.

He just laughs—it's deep and sexy as he swats him away.

"And on that note, I have to get going. Callum, make sure you eat something substantial and promise me you won't drive until later."

He crosses his heart and then pulls me in for a quick hug, and this time, I let him.

"I will, love you," he says into my hair before pulling back.

"Love you too."

Clearing my throat, I look at Liam, suddenly feeling awkward. Do I kiss him on the cheek and say goodbye like I usually would, or do I just wave and make a mad dash for the door?

Before I have time to decide, he does it for me and moves into my space. Lowering his face towards mine, his lips graze my cheek—fuck me, how does he still smell so good after a night on the sofa and with his face between my thighs?

I turn my face enough to kiss his cheek back gently.

When I draw back, I notice I've left a slight lipstick stain, and without thinking, I reach up and quickly rub it away with the pad of my thumb, and I feel his eyes on me. I bristle under his gaze, and it takes everything in my power to not look at him, but I fail miserably.

His eyes are dark, heated even, and I know for my own sanity and the sake of my panties, I need to go and I take a step back.

"Right, bye." My voice cracks as I turn on my heels and head towards the front door.

I can hear Callum saying something to Liam under his breath, and whatever it is has Liam laughing that deep throaty sexy laugh. The one up until yesterday was just his laugh, and now it's tacked on with a side of sex for good measure.

Muttering under my breath, I concentrate on putting one leg in front of the other until I'm at my car.

Inside, I let out a sigh as I buckle my seatbelt and then pull down the sun visor to check my face, which is all kinds of blotchy. Fan-fucking-tastic.

"Get yourself together, Verity, he's just your little brother's best friend."

There's a tap on my window and I let out a startled yelp

and turn to see a grinning Liam. He signals with his finger for me to lower my window. He bends down, his forearm resting on the opening as he leans in, and I find myself tilting my head back.

"What time is your meeting?" he asks.

I just look at him for a few seconds, completely confused by his question.

"At work today, what time is your meeting?"

Oh yeah, right, he renders me all kinds of confused when he's this close.

"It's at one-thirty. Why?"

He doesn't answer me, just removes himself from my open window.

"Drive safe, V." He taps the roof of the car and I watch in my rear-view mirror as he jogs back to the front door. And as if he knew I'd be watching, he glances back over his shoulder and holds up his hand and waves goodbye before disappearing back inside.

Inhaling a deep breath, I start my car and spend the entire journey scolding myself over last night, even though the truth is that it's the best night I've had in a long time, even if it didn't end in sex. I don't know if it was the thrill of being caught, or that it was with Liam, or both.

But I can't remember James ever making me feel that good.

The way Liam worshipped my pussy—his tongue is pure fucking magic. My lower belly flutters to life and I have to squeeze my thighs together to try and dull the ache that builds deep in my core before I'm able to exit my car.

"Morning, Maxine," I say as I approach the front desk.

She looks up from her monitor and smiles, tilting her head to the side. "Morning, hun. What has you looking so flushed?"

I reach for a couple of the leaflets on the counter and wave them over my face, as if it will help rid me of the said flush.

Maxine moves her headset mic away from her mouth as she leans forward on her elbows over the counter.

"Verity, you need to spill, seriously. Did you get some?" she asks.

I look around to make sure no one else is in earshot.

"You could say that."

Her eyes gleam with excitement. "Lunch time, you are going to tell me all about it."

Placing the leaflets back on the stack, I let out a breath. "No can do, I have that stupid lunch meeting."

She pretends to put her fingers in her mouth and gag, because the meeting is with a very pervy line manager, and no one here can stand the guy.

"How about we go for a drink straight after work instead then?"

I nod. "It's a date."

Smiling, I leave her and use my key card to get through the main door that leads to the smaller offices out back. I lost a lot of my so-called friends through association when I split up with James, as if they had to pick sides—pathetic, really. But Maxine and I hit it off as soon as she started working here, and she's become a good friend.

After James and I broke up, a lot of our so-called mutual friends ghosted me. Maxine however has been there for me, as well as my two closest friends, Ali and Sarah. It took me a long time to realise there's a huge difference between friends and acquaintances. And I'm a lot more guarded now than I used to be. James managed to fuck me up in more ways than one.

Chapter Eight

Liam

"Did you see what I mean? She was acting funny, no?" Callum says as he scoops up the runny egg yolk with a chunk of fried bread.

I shrug. "I don't know, man. It probably didn't help that you ate her lunch."

"Whatever. You promise to keep an eye on her for me?"

Whether he asked me or not, I'll look out for her, *always*.

"Yeah, you know I will."

He leans back in his chair and rubs his stomach.

"I needed that. So have you thought anymore about what you want to do work wise?" he asks.

Finishing off my orange juice, I place my glass down and shake my head. "Honestly, I have no idea. There's this career transition workshop I've been thinking of attending."

"Well, there's no rush. And you know if you're strapped for cash, I've got you."

That I have no doubt about, but he knows I won't call in on that offer, even if I was really struggling, but I have enough to see me through for a bit anyway, and staying at his for a couple of weeks saves on what it would have cost in an

Airbnb. My parents wanted me to stay with them in Kent, but that was never going to happen.

"I just need to take a piss and then we'll go," he says, pushing to his feet, the chair squeaking on the wooden floor. I nod and stack our plates and push them to the edge of the table, ready for when the server comes to collect them.

"Hey, can I get the bill please?" I ask when he comes over.

Grabbing the plates, he shakes his head. "The guy you're with already settled the bill."

I smile. "Of course he did."

I thank him and the woman behind the counter and go wait outside, needing to get some air after all that food, and then I pull up the Uber eats app on my phone. After I make my selection, I add in the name and delivery address and place my order and stuff my phone back into my pocket.

"What has you smiling like that?" Callum asks as he joins me outside.

"Nothing. I just ordered Verity some lunch," I tell him as I push off the wall with my foot.

"Shit, why didn't I think of that? Thanks, man, you're a good friend."

Internally, I cringe, because am I a good friend? Isn't it some unsaid cardinal rule that you stay away from your best friend's sister?

Well, it's not something I need to worry about, I'm pretty sure it was just one of those things and I doubt Verity would be interested in a repeat. Besides, didn't I make the decision to act as though it didn't happen and play indifferent? That is, unless she wants to bridge the topic.

"It's cool, it's the least we could do after waking her up," I say, looking in one of the shop windows as we pass.

There's been an eerie quiet to the streets the past couple of days, with worries about this pandemic. And then there's explaining to grown arse adults how to wash their hands and for how long, all with rumours of a lockdown—I'll believe it when I see it.

"So, you'll stay in my room while I'm gone," he says, after he drops me back from picking up my stuff from the hotel and checking out. "Graham and Nick's old room is being decorated and everything from their room is in Carter's old room." I watch as he removes his house keys from his keyring and hands them over.

Callum is the youngest of five, and a total surprise at that. His mum, Linda, was forty-two when she had him. There's a fifteen-year age gap between him and his eldest brother, Carter, and ten years between him and the twins. His dad always joked about their mum getting broody every five years.

They've lived in this three-storey town house since I've known Callum, which has pretty much been forever.

"Do you think they'll consider downsizing when you finally decide to move out?" I ask.

He punches my shoulder. "Hey, they love me living here."

I raise an eyebrow. "Yeah, of course they do."

"It's not like that, man. Even Verity keeps on at me about moving out. I don't know, at least while I'm here I can help them out with bills and there's nothing they can do about it, but the minute I move out, I know they won't accept my money anymore."

Smiling, I look over at him. "Is that why you got them the cruise for their anniversary?"

He nods. "Yeah, Dad had been talking about it for years. I mean, he's seventy, it's not like they're getting any younger. So, I took it into my own hands, otherwise they'd find a way of putting it off."

You've got to give him credit, his heart is in the right place.

"Anyway, wouldn't you prefer to have somewhere of your own for when you want to have company over?"

He laughs at that. "I kind of like that I can use it as a bit of an excuse to be honest, and sometimes, when they realise I still live at home, it's like they're resigned to the fact I'm not boyfriend material."

"Not boyfriend material *yet*," I reiterate. Because I know for a fact someone is going to come along when he least expects it and knock his socks off.

"Sometimes, I wonder how I'm the one who is a romance author and you're not."

I shrug. Truth is, my mum always said I felt too much, and up until I joined the army, I didn't quite understand it, but I sure as hell do now.

"Do you regret it, signing up?" he asks, and I glance away.

"No, but I won't lie, I wish some of the things I've seen I could erase—those things haunt me."

Swallowing, I feel a bead of sweat between my shoulder blades. It's the most open I've been with anyone about my time in the army, but still, I'm not sure I'm ready to say more on the subject.

"It's cool, man, just know I'm here if ever and whenever you want to talk. But promise me that if you're struggling you won't suffer in silence, okay?"

I manage a small smile, because even when I can't form the words, he knows what I need to hear. It's why it's makes my feelings towards Verity so much harder to acknowledge.

"All right then, I guess I should hit the road, at this rate I'll be lucky if I get there by ten."

Standing up, I pull him into a quick hug and then follow him to the door.

"Let me know when you get there, yeah? And drive safe."

Chapter Nine

Verity

"Right, spill," Maxine says as she hands me a glass of wine.

I smile behind the rim of the glass and take a leisurely sip, loving how antsy she gets.

"Let's just say I got way more than I bargained for last night."

She rips open two packets of crisps and slides them into the middle of the table where I reach for one and bring it to my lips.

"So, what the hell happened between work and going home? You go on a tinder date I don't know about?"

Laughing, I shake my head. "You know I haven't got the guts for a dating app."

Maxine rolls her eyes. "V, you only live once. Okay, so Tinder is out of the picture. Are you going to tell me already or make me spend the night asking you questions?"

I love how she doesn't miss a trick, so I put her out of her misery and just tell her but do not go into detail, not even when she asks me about his size, which is easily over five inches, thick and girthy. The memory alone has me blushing like a day caught on the beach without sun protection.

"So, what happens now?" she asks.

Swirling the wine in my glass, I glance up at her. "Nothing," I reply with a shrug. "I think it's best left forgotten."

That and I'm a bloody coward.

"I call bullshit. He sent you lunch, for crying out loud. That's not something someone does who wants to pretend they didn't get good head last night."

Cringing, I look around to see if anyone's in earshot but the pub is surprisingly quiet, probably because so many are starting to panic over the pandemic outbreak in China.

Shaking my head, I snatch up a couple more crisps before she polishes them off.

"No, he's always been thoughtful like that, Callum ate my lunch."

Maxine raises her eyebrows. "That's bullshit. In my experience, a man doesn't do something if he doesn't want to, and if he does, there's generally a meaning behind it."

I lick the salt from my bottom lip. "But he's five years younger than me, and not to mention Callum's best friend."

"And you're older than me, does that mean we can't be friends?"

"No, of course not." Sitting back in my chair, a puff of trapped air escapes the old leather cushion. She wrinkles her nose. "It was the chair," I say, laughing around a sip of my wine.

"Listen, this Liam guy, have you only just had an epiphany and noticed him? And be honest."

Mulling over her question, I think for a moment. "Yes, no, oh I don't know. There's no denying he's hot, but I guess I never saw him in a sexual way before, but walking in on him the way I did, it was like a sudden switch went off."

I play with the crumbs on the tabletop. "It went from zero to a hundred real bloody quick."

Her eyes soften and she gives me a small smile.

"Listen, V, I know everything with James messed you up. His inability to keep his dick in his pants being just one of those things. But you broke up with him for a reason and you've been single for a while now. You're allowed to live a little and enjoy yourself."

Chewing on my lip, I contemplate her words. Part of me knows she's right, however the other part is telling me to tread carefully. There could be serious implications if this all ends badly.

Pulling up on the driveway, I notice Callum's car is gone. There's a light streaming out from the bay window and I take a deep breath before I get out of my car. I'm a grown up, I can be an adult about this. People hook up all the time. Okay, granted, we might not have had full-on sex, but he fucked me with his tongue. And there I go again, thinking of the way he drew an orgasm out of me like he'd been doing it for years.

I stop in my tracks, my laptop bag hitting the side of my knee with a heavy thump.

Because suddenly, I'm thinking about how he learned to do that. I mean, he's clearly not a virgin, but the thought of him being with other women makes me feel anxious, and I don't know why.

Fuck, there's no way I'm jealous, that's ridiculous.

I force myself forward and let myself indoors, trying to be as quiet as possible.

Why the hell are you creeping about?

Stepping into the living room, I'm instantly hit by the smell of... wait... no, it can't be... I follow my nose until I step into the kitchen, where Liam is dishing up a plate of Indian food.

"Oh hey, I got plenty, I didn't know when you'd be home." He adds some rice to his plate. "So I was going to leave it in the fridge for you once it had cooled. Do you want me to dish you some up or have you eaten already?"

I can't help but let out a laugh. Is he rambling?

"No, I haven't, and yes, I'd love some."

Kicking off my heels, I let out a relieved sigh and then pull off my suit jacket. I notice he glances over and then quickly looks away. Compared to him, I feel over dressed and a little bit icky from being at work all day.

"I'll be two secs," I say, holding up my finger and then rushing off upstairs to change into a pair of lounge bottoms. I grab Callum's hoody hanging on the top of the banister. I pull it on over my head and sniff—it doesn't smell like him… maybe Mum used a different washing powder or something? I don't have long to ponder the thought when my stomach grumbles, the delicious smell of the food calling my name.

Back downstairs, my plate is already loaded with all my favourite things and sitting on the coaster is a bottle of beer.

"Thank you." I reach for the bottle and take a small sip.

His eyes trail down to my hoody, his lips curving into a small smile. "You're welcome," he replies, and then he gets stuck in.

I hate to be a cliché, but as soon as the chicken korma passes my lips, I let out a moan of appreciation.

"They do the best takeaway," I say, once I've swallowed the mouthful I'd so ungracefully shoved into my mouth. When I peer over my fork, Liam is watching me with an expression I can't quite decipher.

And then he nods in agreement. "Yeah, I missed it while I was away." He continues eating his food, concentrating on his plate, and just like that, we fall into a relatively comfortable silence, and for now, I'm happy with that… for now.

Chapter Ten

Liam

It was near on impossible for me to eat while she was sitting across from me, making those kinds of noises, and worse, all whilst wearing my hoody. It's just a simple oversized plain white hoody, with a front pocket, that's all it is, and yet, she might as well be in her work suit.

"Thank you for dinner and for my lunch." She stands and begins stacking our plates.

"Any time. Besides, I felt bad we disturbed you when we came back." Shit, if that's not a sure way of saying I am fully aware of what we did, I don't know what is. Needing a second, I reach for the plates and take them through to the kitchen as I glance up at the clock.

"What time did he leave?" she asks, causing me to jump.

I didn't hear her come up behind me. Thankfully, I don't drop the dishes and they just land on the kitchen counter with a loud thump.

"Sorry," she says. "It's my stealthy abilities."

I laugh at that and glance over, watching as she pulls open the dishwasher door before standing to her full height and coming beside me for the dishes, where she stops just shy of my shoulder.

Perfect height ratio for me to tuck her under my arm. It falls silent except for the sounds of the fridge freezer making a low growling sound, and the cutlery as she drops them into the compartment inside the dishwasher.

When she's done, she crosses her arms and glances down and toes at the tiled floor before looking up to find me watching.

She clears her throat. "So, are we going to talk about the elephant in the room?"

I mimic her body language and lean against the kitchen island. So much for me acting indifferent.

Scrubbing my hand over my jaw, I decide to go for honesty.

"If it's an apology you're after, V, you won't get one. I won't insult you by lying because I don't regret it. Not even close."

She opens and closes her mouth a few times before she finds her words, and I wait patiently for her to reply.

"I wasn't asking for an apology, nor do I need one. Even though I was more than complicit, you, on the other hand were drunk…" Her hand moves to her necklace, and she rubs at her locket.

"I was fully aware of everything we did, and I mean *everything*."

"Apart from last night, it would appear the only one in the dark was me." Her cheeks flush.

Shrugging, I say, "Would it have made a difference whether you knew about me getting you the locket, or that I was the stranger you made out with that night?"

Verity digs her teeth into her lower lip. "Yes, no, maybe." She throws up her hands. "I have no idea, and to be honest, it was a lot all at once."

I nod because she's right, of course.

"To be fair, you instigated the kiss on your birthday, and I was more than happy to comply."

My eyes trail down to her necklace, and I hope she doesn't stop wearing it now that she knows it was from me.

"And besides, it was worth keeping it a secret—the locket." I raise my chin in her direction. "Seeing the look on your face and how happy you were when you opened it was worth it."

I push off the island and move towards her. "But tell me, V, honestly, does it make you uncomfortable now you know the truth?"

Her eyes trail a path from my chest up to my face, and she shakes her head.

"Not uncomfortable, but it's complicated. You're you and I'm me, and then there's Callum."

I nod, because truthfully, it's only as complicated as she allows it to be, but if that's how she feels, I'm not about to invalidate her feelings.

"Don't worry, V, I'd never do anything you didn't want me to do."

Reaching out my hand, I touch the locket and roll the pad of my thumb over the warm silver. "We'll be like passing ships in the night. Housemates for a couple of weeks at best. But I don't want you to feel like you need to avoid me, we're both adults. And it changes absolutely nothing about how I feel about you. If anything, it's made my feelings towards you stronger."

Her eyes go wide, and a small breath of air escapes her lips. I step closer, crowding her against the counter, lowering my head and giving her a soft kiss on her cheek before turning on my heels and making my way upstairs to Callum's room.

Closing the door behind me, I lean my head against the door with a thump and let out a deep breath.

Her scent is lingering all around me. It wasn't my intention to get so close to her, but I couldn't help myself.

Everything about her makes me want to let go and be reckless, but we're not on the same page—hell, we're not even on the same book. She's not ready to know just how deep my feelings go, and maybe she never will be.

Kicking off the door, I go sit at Callum's desk and boot up his computer and log in under a guest user. I might as well start looking at sorting my life out somehow. The quicker I have a plan and get myself somewhere to live the better.

Because as much as I want to keep my distance and give Verity space, I also don't. I'm only fucking human, after all. But what I can do is remove myself from the situation so she's not feeling the weight of my feelings, because truth is, now she's had a small glimpse, how much am I going to be able to keep hidden from her, like I did before?

Rubbing my eyes, I crack my neck and look at the time. It's past eleven now and I still haven't heard from Callum. Grabbing my phone off charge, I send him a quick text.

Me: You get there okay, man?

Stepping out into the hallway, I laugh to myself as I scroll through TikTok and head downstairs. The television is on low, and it's only when I approach to turn it off and glance to the sofa, I see Verity has fallen asleep. I'm torn between leaving her be, waking her, or carrying her upstairs to her room.

She's always been quite a deep sleeper, not that I should know that, and I'm aware it's creepy as fuck, but sod it.

Sliding one arm under her knees and the other at the top of her shoulders, I pull her up to my chest. Her eyelids flutter and she lets out the tiniest noise but otherwise remains sleeping.

I pull back her duvet and carefully place her on the mattress. Just as I cover her, she mumbles something about not liking marmite and I have to stifle my laugh.

Switching off her lamp, I close her door behind me and go

back downstairs and check my phone on the way to the kitchen.

Callum: Literally just pulled up, I'm beat. I'll touch base with you in a day or two.

Switching on the kettle, I look through the cupboard until I find the chamomile tea.

"Bingo."

Here's to hoping I'll get some sleep tonight. Apart from the couple of hours with Verity last night, I've been struggling to sleep at night, and honestly, it's beginning to take its toll. Cat naps during the day can only sustain you for so long before it begins catching up on you.

Chapter Eleven

Verity

It doesn't take a genius to work out that Liam carried me to bed last night, *again*. I guess I should be grateful, but I mean, I'm a grown arse woman, he could have just woken my sorry arse.

As soon as I'm showered and dressed, I go downstairs to make myself a coffee to go. I barely woke up without my alarm—thank goodness for the body clock, I guess.

It's only as I'm making my way through the living room, I glimpse Liam stretched out on the sofa again. Looks like I'm not the only one who fell asleep there last night.

Gingerly, I walk over and give myself a moment to take him in. His hand is just below the waistband of his joggers, his T-shirt has risen, showing off some of his abs, and I itch to reach out and touch him.

"I can feel you watching me," he says, his voice thick from sleep.

I startle and cover my chest with my hand, my heart jack-hammering against my breastplate.

His lips curve into a smile as he looks up at me.

"You're not funny. What if I would have been holding a hot drink?"

He pushes himself up and throws his legs off the sofa. "You weren't, I heard you come downstairs."

I watch as he runs his fingers through his hair and almost want to swat his hand away and do it for him. Fuck, he looks delicious in the morning.

Squeezing my thighs together, I turn my back on him before I really make myself late for work.

"You're cutting it fine this morning," he calls out to my retreating back.

I pause my hand on my travel mug. "Either you're really observant or that's kind of creepy," I say over my shoulder, and he joins me in the kitchen and grabs a pint of milk from the fridge before getting himself a mug.

"I'll choose observant," he says with a playful wink.

My nails tap on my parents' granite workshop.

"You know, a watched pot never boils," he says, scooping some coffee granules into his mug.

"Yeah, well, it's a kettle, and it will momentarily."

He lets out a gruff laugh that I feel deep in my belly. Shit, if this is how the next couple of weeks will be, then I am in serious fucking trouble.

My phone pings with a text and I open it.

Maxine: Gah, everyone is freaking out about this coronavirus, hurry up and get here. Nick is being extra obnoxious. And I need saving from these gossip mongers.

I shake my head.

Me: You're the biggest gossip of all!

The kettle clicks and Liam reaches it before I do, making my coffee exactly how I like it before making his own.

Maxine: Not when it comes to the important things xox

Which is true, Maxine has always had my back.

"Thank you," I say to Liam, picking up my mug and screwing on the lid.

"Always a pleasure, V."

I lean over and kiss his cheek. "Bye," I croak out, making a beeline towards the front door, snatching my laptop bag off the small table in the entryway before darting out the door.

Maxine wasn't kidding when she said everything was going crazy about the announcement due later this evening—hence why I'm home early.

When I let myself in, I glance over and catch Liam startle in the armchair just as I close the front door behind me.

His hand goes to his chest as he wipes his other hand over his jaw.

"Sorry," I say.

"No, it's fine, I haven't been sleeping and I was taking a five-minute catnap." He glances to his watch and then back to me. "You're home early."

I kick off my heels and walk into the living room and plonk myself down on the sofa.

"Yeah, one of my managers was getting all antsy over the PM's announcement, so he sent us all home early."

Not that I'm complaining. Who doesn't like a half day?

I push back to my feet. "In fact, there's a bottle of wine chilling in the fridge and a bath bomb and a bath calling my name."

Liam's Adam's apple is prominent as he swallows. Giving me a tight smile, he stands too, and I have to tilt my head back to look at his face. Am I getting shorter?

"I think I'll go for a run."

We both move towards the stairs at the same time, and I let out a nervous laugh. "After you. I need to grab that wine I was talking about anyway."

I can hear him moving around upstairs as I remove the

cork and pour myself a large glass of Prosecco, and then I dig in the freezer for the frozen strawberries and plop one in there too. Such a neat trick to keep it cold without watering it down.

Taking a small sip, the bubbles tickle my nose and I almost choke before swallowing as Liam appears in a small pair of shorts and a running vest.

Fuck!

"See you in a while, enjoy your bath," he says over his shoulder with barely a glance in my direction as he hurries out of the door. That's weird.

Upstairs, I start running my bath as I strip out of my clothes and toss them in the linen bin and tie my hair in a tight bun. And then I grab my dressing gown and a book off my dresser and lock myself in the bathroom.

Once everything is on the bath rack, I climb in and sink into the water and let out a sigh.

I pull up my Terrible Trio group chat with my best friends, Ali and Sarah, trying to decide if I should mention what happened with Liam. After all, they've known him as long as they've known me.

Fuck it.

Me: Hey ladies, you okay?

I'm surprised when Ali is the first to reply, especially since she had her second baby, her time is precious.

Ali: Tired, but nothing unusual there. *Sends a picture of her hair in a top knot and her T-shirt inside out* How about you?

Sarah: Hey, I'm alive, how's it been being back at your mum and dad's?

Me: Let's just say I got way more than I bargained for *blush emoji*

Ali: Someone's being vague?!

Sarah: Don't keep us hanging...

A nervous swarm of butterflies erupts in my stomach as I type a response.

Me: Okay, so you know Liam, Callum's best friend?
Ali: Of course.
Sarah: Yeah, he's so dreamy.

I burst out laughing at that. Sarah has never been one to shy away from saying what she thinks out loud, married or not.

Me: Yep, the one and only. Anyway, it turns out he's staying here for a few weeks in Callum's room while he's away. But the thing is, me and him might have gotten up to something the other night.
Ali: Might have or did?
Me: Did *embarrassed emoji*
Sarah: You go girl. Was he any good? Oh, I bet he's hung like a horse.
Ali: Seriously, Sarah? *eyeroll*
Sarah: Oh, come on, you were thinking the same, I know you always thought he had a nice arse.
Ali: Verity, spill the beans already...

I tell them what happened, but don't go into graphic detail. I know if we were in person, Sarah would pry it out of me, she has this uncanny ability of getting all the details.

Sarah: Damn that's hot *flame emoji*
Ali: You go girl.
Me: Yeah, it was hot, and do you know what? It felt good.
Sarah: Don't get stuck in your head, Verity. I know what you're like, and if you want more, then you take Liam by the balls. You hear me?
Ali: What Sarah is saying is do what makes you happy, and if that means hot sex with Liam, then so be it.
Me: Thank you, love you both xox
Sarah: Love you too xox
Ali: Love you three xox

By the time I'm officially prune status, I pull the plug out and drain the last of my wine, feeling pleasantly buzzed. Once the water passes my knees, I get out, dry off, and pull on my dressing gown. I spend a good ten-minutes moisturising and then pull on my lounge bottoms and tank top, but then last minute, I grab the hoody and slip it on again. *Maybe my mum did switch washing powder?* I think, as I make my way downstairs with my empty glass.

I look at the clock and wonder where Liam is. Surely he can't still be out running? And then, as if by magic, the doorbell chimes.

Looking out of the window, Liam holds up his hand and I open the door.

"Sorry, forgot my key."

Moving aside, he enters, smelling sweaty, and as if it's possible as sexy as hell.

"Perfect timing," I say.

He smiles, brushing his damp hair away from his brow.

Hooking his thumb over his shoulder, he starts walking backwards. "I'm going to go shower. The last thing you need is my stink ruining your time in the bath."

He turns and runs up the stairs two at a time.

My cheeks begin to heat because it was the last thing I was thinking, and now the image of him naked in the shower swims in my mind. I only had the privilege of seeing his cock, and I'd be lying if secretly I didn't want to see more.

Chapter Twelve

Liam

There was absolutely no way I was staying in the house while she was up there taking a bath, and it didn't help that I'd woken up all discombobulated from a nightmare either. They usually don't happen when I nap in the day, but maybe being tired is beginning to seriously take its toll.

But when she answered the door, fresh out of the bath, smelling good enough to eat, it took everything in me to keep my sweaty paws away from her. If anything, she's now given me a hankering for mango—it might even be worth nipping out to the shop to grab a carton of mango juice.

I try not to think about her while I'm in the shower, but it's impossible. If I thought I had it bad before, it's nothing now I've had a taste.

My dick is rock hard, desperate for release, and I know if I don't take care of it now, there is no way I'll be able to go near her without it making itself known.

Fisting my cock, I rest my forehead against the tiled wall and close my eyes as the spray from the shower runs down my spine.

The vivid memory of her above me as I fucked her with my tongue makes my mouth water. How she sounded, the way she felt with her mouth wrapped around my hard shaft as she smothered my face with her pussy, the way she fluttered around my tongue as her climax was cresting, it was a sensory fucking overload.

I speed up, working my wrist in just the right rhythm as my breathing picks up, the image of her hands on me instead of mine. My balls pull up tight and my spine tingles right before I explode all over my hand and the shower wall. It spurts out in quick succession, and I let out a deep groan, throwing my head back, my breathing heavy as I let myself relish in the moment.

After I've showered and changed, I make my way downstairs, wondering what to have for dinner, but when I walk into the kitchen, I stop in my tracks. Verity is swaying her hips as she sings along to the radio, a spatula in hand as a makeshift microphone. She always was amazing when it came to karaoke.

I sound like a dying animal, but her and her brothers it would seem don't have that problem. Callum can play the guitar and Verity the piano. My mum sent me for music lessons during the summer holidays, but it was clear after a week it was not, nor would it ever be my calling. Instead, I joined a summer swimming club and loved it. I've always found being in the water peaceful, even now.

I can't help but allow my gaze to roam down the length of Verity's body as she wiggles, her sock covered feet sliding along the tiled floor.

When she turns to grab something from the cupboard, she spots me and flings the spatula in my direction. Thankfully, my reflexes are good, and I duck out of the way.

"Shit, sorry," she says, laughing as I pick up the spatula and wash it under the tap.

"Now who's being stealthy?" I say, giving her a wink.

Her cheeks heat and she tucks some of her hair behind her ear that's fallen from her bun.

"There's being stealthy and there's being sneaky," she retorts, snatching the utensil from my fingers.

"What's cooking?" I ask, leaning my hip against the counter, her soft mango fragrance drifting over me.

"Chicken and orzo, and don't worry, I made plenty."

My stomach grumbles, and I realise other than breakfast I haven't eaten anything else today. I really need to get my life back on track.

"Can I do anything?" I look around.

She tilts her head to the cutlery drawer. "You could set the table. Also, there is a bottle of red in the wine rack if you want to open it and let it breathe."

It's not long before she carries in the pan and sets it in the middle of the table on the heat proof mat and then comes back with a plate of garlic bread.

"Tuck in," she says. "Hey, do you mind if I switch on the TV so we can catch the announcement?"

I shake my head, my mouth already full, and she springs up to grab the remote and brings it back. They have a TV in their dining room and their living room, not to mention in their bedrooms. It's a little weird for me, because growing up, my parents had the one television—even now. And you weren't allowed to watch it until after dinner, and never in the morning, that was a huge hell no.

Thank goodness for mobiles, that's all I can say.

I look up the length of the table to the far wall, where the widescreen is hung as it blares to life.

Verity cringes and quickly turns it down. "I swear, if I didn't know better, I'd say one of my parents is having hearing issues. The amount of times I've had the television or the radio near on give me a heart attack is ridiculous."

I smile as she turns it over to the BBC.

We both listen to the PM speak as the headlines scroll continuously along the bottom of the screen while we dive into our food.

"Fucking hell, V. I never knew you could cook this well," I say as I shovel another forkful of chicken into my mouth.

She laughs. "Why would you? My mum never lets me near the kitchen when I'm here."

And it's a stark reminder that for the last five years she's been sharing a house with another man.

"Now is the time for everyone to stop non-essential contact and travel."

Boris Johnson's voice echoes in the background.

Verity pauses with a piece of bread at her lips, and I try my hardest not to stare, but it's impossible. It's only when her eyes roam to mine, I realise she asked me a question.

"What do you think this means? Is it likely we'll have to go into a full lockdown?" And it's not hard to hear the worry in her voice.

I nod. "It's very possible."

"As much as I hate to admit it, it's really scary," she admits quietly, before taking a bite of her garlic bread. Before I can stop myself, I reach out and touch her arm, setting my nerves on end when she looks to my hand then back to my face.

"It is, but at least they're looking at taking extra measures, so that's good."

Her phone rings and causes her to drop her fork. Rolling her eyes, she answers a facetime call.

"Hey, Callum." She props the phone on its pop socket and picks up her fork.

"Hi. What are you eating?"

"Chicken and orzo," I say. Verity angles the phone so we're both in view.

"Oh, hey, man," Callum says, pouting. "I love your chicken and orzo," he whines.

"You snooze you lose," Verity says, humming around a mouthful of food, and it takes everything in me to focus on Callum and not her.

"Why you are wearing that?" he says, nodding to the hoody she's been donning for the past two nights. My eyes glance to Verity as she looks down then back to him.

"Because it's super comfortable," she says with a smirk.

"You want to be careful, man, she won't batter an eyelid about half inching that and keeping it for herself." Her mouth drops open as she looks to me and then back to Callum, her whole face now flushing red.

Chapter Thirteen

Verity

"I thought it was yours," I say to Callum.

He shakes his head. "Nope, it's Liam's."

I place my cutlery down on the side of my plate and push my chair back, reaching for the hem of the hoody.

"What the fuck, Verity?" Callum says dramatically, covering his eyes.

Pausing, I look at him incredulously. "I have a tank top on underneath, Callum, for fuck's sake."

Liam reaches out, his hand hot as he touches the back of mine. "It's fine, keep it on," he says, and I notice I'm not the only one flushed.

"Anyway, striptease averted," Callum says, and I'm quick to give him the middle finger. "I just wanted to see if you saw the news?"

"Yeah, we saw," Liam says, and I push my plate away, no longer hungry. He glances at my plate and frowns before looking back to Callum.

"Nice bruise, by the way." Liam lets out a deep chuckle that has my belly fluttering.

I lean forward, and sure enough, he's sporting an egg on his head. "Have you been fighting?" I ask. "Please tell me you haven't. Less than two days away and you're already causing trouble with the locals."

Callum throws his head back and laughs, and so does Liam.

"Nah. Put it this way, Reggie one, Callum zero."

I look between the two of them. What am I missing? "Who is Reggie?"

"A dildo," answers Liam for him.

"What the hell? I don't want to hear anymore." I quickly cover my ears but hear Callum's muffled reply as Liam pulls one of my hands away.

"Eww, no, it's not like that, you perv." He rolls his eyes. "There was a mix up with the booking, so when I let myself in and went to the bedroom, Quinn thought I was an intruder, and in a blind panic, she walloped me with her dildo, Reggie."

I cover my mouth with my hand, not sure what part is worse, unable to stop my laughter. Not only did she name her battery-operated friend, but she also used it as a weapon of choice, and on my brother of all people. This is priceless.

My sides are aching when I'm finally able to catch my breath again.

"Where is she now?" I question.

Callum gives a wistful smile. "Here. I'll sort out other arrangements tomorrow."

"Such a gentleman," I say, holding my hand over my heart, and now it's his turn to flip me the bird.

"Whatever. I'll call you and let you know once I sort out somewhere else to stay."

Liam reaches over for my plate. "Are you finished?" he asks quietly.

I nod and he takes it with his and turns towards the direction of the kitchen.

"Or you could just come home?" I offer, my eyes trained on Liam's arse, hugged by his grey joggers. Lord, give me strength.

Callum replies, but I only catch the tail end.

"Fair enough," I say, hoping it's enough to not drop myself in it.

"Okay, well, I'm going to go, speak to you later."

I pick up my phone. "Okay, love you, bye."

"Love you too. Bye, Liam," he shouts out as I quickly end the call.

Liam comes back in and reaches for his glass and finishes his wine before tilting his chin towards mine. "Do you want a top up?" he asks.

Bringing mine to my lips, I down the last mouthful.

"Why not."

He half fills our glasses. "Thanks for dinner, it was lovely. I put the rest in a container, thought you could have it for lunch tomorrow."

"No worries, and thanks." He's so bloody attentive it makes my teeth hurt, but in the sweetest way.

"Did you already know about Reggie?" I ask.

He nods. "Of course. Me and Callum tell each other everything," he replies.

My jaw drops and I raise my eyebrows. He clears his throat, shaking his head.

"With the exception of us," he says, pointing between us.

I repeat the word '*us*' in my head, looking down at my feet and then back to him.

"I can't believe you never told me I was wearing your hoody." I feel like such an idiot, no wonder he was smirking at me the other night when I came downstairs wearing it.

His eyes trail a path from my face down to my chest and back up again. Flames lick my skin in his wake. I might be covered in fabric, but in this moment, I might as well be naked in his presence.

He stuffs his hands into his pockets, the weight pulling the waistband of his joggers lower.

"I like seeing you wearing my clothes," he admits, his eyes

a dark marble blue, and full of desire. Even if I wanted to believe otherwise, the chemistry between us is palpable, there's no denying it. "Does it bother you now you know it's mine?"

"Depends. Would you have told me?"

His lips lift into the ghost of a smile as he takes a step closer, removing his hands from his pockets.

"Eventually," he says. Reaching out, he grips the front pocket of the hoody, causing my heart rate to accelerate. Leaning down to my ear, his breath tickles my flesh when he whispers, "But I would enjoy helping you out of it, that I can promise you."

I swallow and lick my lips, hating that I sound so breathless even to my own ears. His hands move until they're at the hem of the hoody and move underneath, until I feel the faintest touch of his fingertips as they travel over my bare flesh.

My lower stomach clenches with excitement as my nipples rub against my tank top. His fingers tighten, digging in ever so slightly, not enough to hurt but enough for him to hold me still.

"Would you enjoy that, V? Me helping you out of *my* hoody?"

Oh my God.

Of course I would. Who wouldn't in their right mind want that? Has he not seen himself? If you looked up tall, dark, and handsome in the dictionary, there he'd be. The tip of his tongue touches my earlobe and I startle. And then he surprises the fuck out of me when he sucks it into his mouth, sending sparks of electricity throughout my entire body, causing a tingling sensation all over, and I shiver.

"Fuck," I hiss out through my teeth.

He draws back, but not enough for me to see his face, his lips pressed against the shell of my ear.

"That wasn't an answer, Verity."

I try to focus and pull all my brain cells back to a functioning state, but it's near on impossible as I attempt to stutter a coherent sentence and I squeeze my eyes closed tightly.

He steps back and I miss his warmth immediately, causing my eyes to spring open.

"It's okay. I've waited this long; I can wait a little longer."

And then he turns around and walks off into the kitchen, leaving me standing there completely lost for words.

What just happened?

Chapter Fourteen

Liam

Shit. I run my hand through my hair and pace the length of the kitchen. I just can't stay away from her, and yet, I still don't know if she wants me, and the thought of pushing her into something and her regretting it is not something I want to even contemplate. I already crossed a line with her the other night—fuck, maybe I should cut my losses and just leave her alone? I pretty much told her I've been waiting for her. Shit.

Busying myself, I rinse off the plates and pan before landing them into the dishwasher, and then wipe down the counters. When I walk back into the living room, she's sipping her wine in one hand and scrolling through her phone with her thumb in the other. I step towards her and open my mouth to say something, anything, but then I think better of it and make myself scarce instead, heading up to Callum's room.

I think it's safe to say she pretty much knows how I feel, so maybe I should just let the chips fall where they may, and she might just be the one coming to me.

Needing to stop obsessing over the situation, I login to the computer and start looking at possible options of what to do next. I can't keep sofa—or better still bedroom-surfing, for that matter. I have money saved, so I'm not worried about that so much at the minute, but still, I need to do something.

Joining the army as a combat medical technician pushed me in ways I never could have imagined. But mostly, I learnt so much about myself I don't think I would have if I hadn't joined. But I do know I thrive on helping others, and it's probably why I feel useless at the moment. I tend to adapt well to my environment, and as conceited as it might sound and for the most part, I have always worked well under pressure, until I didn't, of course.

I still feel as though I'm to blame. Even though I know there was nothing I could have done, it's the survivor guilt, a significant symptom of PTSD so I've been told, and yet, it doesn't make it any easier.

It's why the nightmares come, and why sleeping at night is becoming a real issue lately.

I dig around in Callum's desk drawer and pull out a notepad and pen. At least he's never short of notebooks.

Opening the first page, staring at me is a hand drawn penis, and I can't help but laugh. Stupid really, considering I am a grown arse man.

So, I turn to the next page only to see stick figures in all kinds of precarious positions, and sure enough, the more I flick through the more I come across.

Grabbing my phone, I take a picture and send it to Callum.

Me: Mate, not sure what exactly I stumbled across here, but did you want to talk about it?

I lay my phone beside me and type in King's College London and then search for degrees.

The desk vibrates and my phone moves, alerting me to a text.

Callum: Oh, those are my why choose stick men. Sometimes I just need a visual of how a position might work.

Me: Wow, okay, well, it's probably a good thing you're an author because your drawing skills leave a lot to be desired.

My phone rings, and even without looking at the screen, I'd know it was him about to roast me for my last message.

I swipe to answer, and his head appears.

"Fuck off, man."

I smile. "Hello to you too," I reply.

"Yeah, hey, man. What you doing rifling around in my drawers anyway? And maybe avoid my bottom drawer."

I can't help but laugh at that. "Believe me, I have no intention of going there. I'm just looking at degrees and needed a pad."

"Oh, second drawer down, there's a fresh one, it's all yours." He holds up two fingers as though I can't count to two.

So I flip him off, and he just throws his head back and laughs.

"How's Verity? Is she doing all right?"

I bounce my leg up and down. "Yeah, she's okay, from what I can tell." Needing to divert the conversation, I find a new subject matter. "Anyway, any more incidents with a dildo you want to tell me about?" I say, wiggling my eyebrows.

He shakes his head and rubs the invisible spot on his forehead. "No, that fucker hurt. But there might have been an incident with a shower door. Hey, what do you think about me getting a tattoo?" he says deadpan.

I can't help it, I throw my head back and laugh. "You? A tattoo? Unless it's a fake one, yeah, I can't see it somehow."

"Well, I'm not talking huge or anything."

Callum, who is shit scared of needles and looks as though he will pass out just from the sound of a tattoo gun—yeah, I don't think so.

"I'd have to see it to believe it. Anyway, what brought this on?"

I prop my phone up in the holder he has fixed to his desk and start scrolling for the degree courses.

"Just saw something that made me think I want one is all."

Looking up from the keyboard, I raise an eyebrow. "Does this have anything to do with a blonde bombshell you're rooming with?"

His cheeks begin to heat, and I stop what I'm doing to give him my full attention.

"Well, well, well, this is interesting."

"What is?" he asks as he climbs into his car.

"You really like this girl, don't you?"

He throws his head back against the headrest and rubs his palm over his jaw. "Mate, she's not like anyone I've ever met before. There's just something about her, I don't know what it is, because it's not just one thing, it's everything."

Opening his eyes, he looks back at me. "I really think we could have something, you know?"

I can't help my smile, cause damn if he isn't smitten.

"Then go for it, you have nothing to lose and everything to gain."

Biting his lower lip, he sits up a little straighter and then slaps the steering wheel with one hand.

"Do you know what? You're right."

"Of course I am. When have I ever led you astray?"

His face turns serious and I look away, my eyes tracking the framed pictures of his published books.

"Listen, I didn't know it was sharpie, okay? Will you ever let that go?"

I glance back and his eyebrows are almost to his hairline. "Doubtful. I had to walk around with a penis on the side of my face for a week, Liam, a week."

Tucking my lips between my teeth, I try not to laugh. "Oh, come on, you did write Callum's bitch on my stomach," I retort.

"Yeah, but you could easily hide that."

His mum threw away all the sharpies after that. Worse part was they had a funeral on the Sunday and Verity had to use her expensive makeup to cover it up for the day.

He makes a fake gagging sound. "I still can't go near Jack Daniels." His face takes on a greenish tinge.

I let out an involuntary shudder. "No, man, me neither."

After another five minutes of chatting shit, we say our goodbyes and we hang up. I click on the Physiotherapy BSc and then order a prospectus. One day at a time.

Chapter Fifteen

Verity

I've hardly seen Liam this past week—between me being at work and then coming home, we're like passing ships in the night, and if anything, he's quiet, withdrawn even. I hear him moving around at night and most mornings I find him asleep on the couch. It doesn't take a genius to work out he's struggling since leaving the army.

It's why I got him the gift, the one I've had sitting in a bag in my room. I bring it downstairs with me and place it on the counter as I enter the kitchen.

"Hi," I say, coming up beside him. He already has my favourite mug down and is filling it with coffee, making it the exact way I like it without even having to ask.

"Morning," he replies, giving me a genuine smile as he stirs my coffee and slides it over to me.

"Thank you. You're up early." And then I instantly regret my comment. "God, that sounded wrong, fuck. Sorry, I'm not implying you're lazy."

I close my mouth, knowing that whatever else spews from my lips is going to be a load of waffle cock.

He laughs. "I know you weren't, it's cool."

Fuck it, it's now or never.

"So, hmm, I have something for you," I say, my voice cracking slightly, causing him to frown. "And I hope you don't take it the wrong way."

I reach over for the bag and slide it towards him on the counter. His eyes scan between the bag and me, and his hand moves toward it, but I quickly stop him.

"Promise you won't be offended, or get mad?"

He looks slightly perplexed. To be fair, I would be too, it's not like I'm making much sense.

"I promise, unless it's deodorant and you've been holding out on telling me I smell," he says deadpan.

I smile and shake my head. "No, I love how you smell."

Shit, I just said that out loud.

"Anyway…" I point at the bag.

I watch as he pulls out the contents—colouring pens, and a colouring book. He's quiet as he reads the front and then turns it over to look at the back before flipping it back over again.

"Do you remember how growing up you always used to draw pictures and do a lot of colouring in?"

He nods as he turns the book over in his hands.

"Well, I know you've been struggling to sleep, and I thought this might help, you know? It's good for anxiety and other things…"

"And PTSD. You can say it, and it's something I am getting help for, but this," he says, holding it up in the air. "Was really thoughtful, thank you."

I let out a breath. "So, you're not mad? You don't think I overstepped?"

He shakes his head, his cheeks tinging with red. "Of course not, it was sweet of you to think of me. It means a lot that you'd go out your way for me like that, thank you."

"It was hardly going out of my way, I just thought it might help. I do care about you, Liam."

My eyes are drawn to his lips as his tongue flicks over the

bottom one. To distract myself, I blow on my coffee before taking a small sip and smacking my lips together. I need to keep distracting myself from where my mind is going. "Hey, if you ever needed a job, you could always be my own private barista."

His eyes crinkle in amusement with his smile. "Coffee on tap, you'd be a bloody live wire. Do you still cut yourself off before six?" he asks.

"Yeah. Wait, how do you know that?"

Reaching out, he taps my nose with his finger. "That's for me to know and you to find out."

The smallest of gestures sends tingles to my lower belly. Clearing my throat, I find myself having to look away.

"Hey there's another announcement from Boris tonight, are you going to be home?" he asks before bringing his mug to his lips, and I can't help but feel mesmerised as they touch the rim—he has such kissable lips.

Oh my God, I need to stop this.

"Yeah, I'll be here. Maybe my boss will send us all home early again? Everyone is already pushing for working from home, but I know what he's like, he'll wait until it's announced."

His phone chimes and he pulls it from his back pocket, swiping his screen, music plays, and I quirk an eyebrow.

"Sorry, I'm totally hooked on TikTok. Are you on there?"

I shake my head. Maxine is, and I swear she can literally lose hours being engrossed on that app.

"Here." He turns the screen for me to see.

There's a dog being held by a man as it struggles to get free, and the camera zooms out to a man on a stretcher as the dog goes and lies on his stomach.

"Oh my God, Liam." I swat his shoulder, feeling my eyes prick with tears. "Not what I need to see first thing in the morning, I'm already emotional."

He pulls his phone away and instantly grips my chin, tilting my face so I have to look at him.

"Why? Who's upset you?" His jaw clenches, his eyes dark but not in a desire filled way I've witnessed before. Now he looks pissed.

Wow, he went Bucky Barnes to Winter Soldier real fucking quick.

I reach up and touch the back of his hand. "No one, I'm fine, honestly."

He studies my face. "I don't believe you."

Licking my lips, I swallow before replying. "I promise, it's no one, if you must know I always get a little extra emotional leading up to my period."

I expect him to scrunch up his nose or change the subject like James always did, but instead his eyes soften.

"Oh, I'm sorry. Is there anything I can do to make you feel better? Do you need me to run out and get you anything today?"

Seriously, could he be any sweeter? "No but thank you. Wow, Liam Carmichael, you're going to make some girl happy someday, and they'll be lucky to have you."

He blinks as though whatever spell he was just under broke, and he strokes his thumb over my cheek before dropping his hand and taking a step back, and like before, I miss his touch instantly and I hate that the look he had only moments ago has been replaced with one of sadness.

What is it with me saying all the wrong things around him? I need a girl chat with Maxine, and stat. With that, he makes quick work of rushing off, and I return to my room to get dressed before I go. I can't help but feel like I hurt his feelings somehow, and it wasn't my intention.

Approaching my brother's bedroom door, I tap on it with the back of my knuckle.

"Yeah," he calls out. I push it open and he moves to his feet from the bed and comes towards me in two purposeful strides, and then before I even have a chance to speak, he grabs the back of my neck, lowers his face, and kisses me.

I'm so stunned at first, I don't react, and then when my back hits the wall with a soft thump, I come back to myself and part my lips, allowing him access. I feel him smile right before his tongue teases mine. This kiss is even better than the other ones we shared, which is a testament in itself.

My hands move up to his chest, then up and over his shoulders as I wrap them around his neck and pull him closer. I can feel his hard length pressing against me, wishing there wasn't this tight as hell pencil skirt between us, otherwise, I'm pretty sure my legs would be wrapped around him too.

A deep groan of pleasure works its way up through his chest and into my mouth.

I don't know how long he kisses me pressed up against the wall, but when he pulls back, we're both out of breath, and if my eyes are anything like his, I feel as dazed as he looks.

Then he pins me with his stare. "For the record, Verity, true disclosure, I want you to be *that* girl. And I want to be the one to make *you* happy."

Well, shit!

"It's okay, I don't expect you to say anything, this isn't the same for you as it is for me. But just so you know, going forward, I won't keep holding back."

Chapter Sixteen

Liam

Her mouth opens and closes like a fish out of water, as if she's trying to articulate a response, but like I said, I don't need it, I just needed her to know.

"Okay then," she finally manages, her lips forming a shy but thoroughly kissed smile.

"Yeah?" I ask, making sure I heard her right and it's not just my ears playing tricks on me.

She nods. "Yeah, but bear with me, okay? This is all"—she waves her hands between us—"beyond surreal."

"I can do that."

Never have words given me so much hope.

Hooking her thumb over her shoulder, she says, "I really should get going."

The thought of letting her go, even for a moment, causes a deep ache in my chest, but this is real, it's happening. This is not some warped part of my imagination making this shit up.

"Okay, drive safe."

Her eyes sparkle, her smile even brighter than before.

"I will. Bye, Liam."

She goes onto her tiptoes and gives me a kiss—what she probably intended to be a chaste one, but I deepen it and tug her to my body, making sure to give her a proper goodbye kiss.

"See you later, V."

Her cheeks are the most beautiful shade of red, and I can't help the swarm of pride that hits me in the chest. I did that. Reluctantly, I release her and let her go. Part of me wants to trail after her and follow her like a loyal puppy, but I don't want to push my luck. I've already come on pretty strong as it is, but when she knocked on the door and entered looking wounded, my little piece for self-restraint I had left snapped.

I need to get rid of some of this excess energy and go for a run. When she's back from work, I have every intention of worshipping her in any capacity she will allow.

Maybe it's a little presumptuous of me, but I'm cooking us both dinner tonight. The past week I think we were both avoiding one another in our own ways, and I have every intention of making that up to her this evening, at least before the announcement, which I am ninety-nine percent sure will indeed be Boris announcing lockdown measures. To what degree, I have absolutely no idea, but in a few hours, we'll find out.

I don't care if it's too much, I set the table and even found her mum's candle stick holders and some candles. I light them and give the table a once over. Fuck, the candles make it way too romantic, and if I was worried about scaring her off, that will do the damn trick.

But just as I'm about to extinguish the flames, I hear the rattle of her keys clanging against the door before the sound of it opening.

I watch as she kicks off her heels, her eyes dancing over the table as she walks towards me. The dining room and living room are open-plan, so it's not hard to see the table when she walks in.

"Wow, what's the occasion? Is someone getting lucky tonight?"

Swallowing hard, I shake my head. "Oh, shit, no." I panic, worried she thinks this is just a way for me to get her into bed. I lean over and suck in a breath to blow out the candle when her hand presses down on my forearm.

"I was joking. This is lovely. Did you cook for us?"

I nod and let out a breath as I turn to face her, waiting to see what she does next. She doesn't disappoint when she goes up on her tiptoes, her intentions clear as she meets my mouth for a kiss.

"I could get used to that," I admit as I pull back, one hand on her hip, the other splayed across her lower back. I dare not let my hand drift any lower, as I really do want to feed her and worship her in any way she'll permit me to tonight. A kiss like this is enough, but I didn't have any expectations. She asked me to bear with her and I intend on doing just that.

"Me too." Her cheeks heat and she glances away before looking back to me, a nervous giggle escaping her. "Sorry, this is going to take some getting used to."

Tucking her hair behind her ear, I smile. "It's okay, we'll go at your speed. I'm just here for the ride," I say and can't help but wiggle my eyebrows at the use of my own pun, hoping it settles her somewhat.

"I also got you some bits," I say, pointing to the small tub on the coffee table in the living room.

She lets go of me and walks over and has a look.

When I was buying dinner, I made a point to get her all of her favourite comfort things.

"Wow, what is this?" Her hands start pulling some of the contents out. "Heat pads, chocolates, oh, a bath bomb." She brings it to her nose and lets out a contended sigh. "Hmm, that's one of my favourites." There's a pair of fluffy socks, some herbal tea, sweet treats, face mask, anything I could get that she might like.

"Oh my God, Liam, is this a period care package?"

I look away, feeling a little embarrassed now. It's super fucking intimate and I'm not even her boyfriend, *yet*.

But maybe, deep down, I want her to see how good I can be for her, not just today, but always.

"Hey." She steps up to me and wraps her arms around my waist. "That's beyond sweet, I love it." Pulling back, she looks up at my face and smiles. "I can't believe you got me all my favourites too."

Not going to lie, I don't want her to see me as just sweet, but I also do. I've spent years longing after her and saying all the things I would do if ever I was given the opportunity, even if the chances were slim. So now, while I can, I sure as hell will.

The timer goes off on the oven and I lean down, kissing her forehead. "Go on, dinner will be ready in about twenty minutes if you want to get changed."

She takes hold of my hand and squeezes softly. I love how soft and velvety her touch is.

"It's a little alarming how well you know me, and yet, I feel like I'm barely scratching the surface with you."

"You can ask me anything and I'll answer."

Now she's the one wiggling her eyebrows. "Oh, anything?"

I nod and pull her closer, lifting her off her feet as I give her a quick kiss before placing her on her feet again.

"Yes, anything."

Spinning her so her back is to my chest, I coax her to move and then give her arse a playful slap.

"Now this could be fun," she says over her shoulder before disappearing upstairs.

Chapter Seventeen

Verity

Holy shit, he made me a period care package. That seriously has to be the sweetest thing ever. I quickly get changed and pull on his hoody. Now I know how much he likes seeing me in his clothes, it's the least I can do after what he just did.

Me: Guess what Liam did...

I go to the bathroom and wet a makeup remover pad under running water before wringing it out and wiping off my makeup. Pausing, I stare at my reflection. Even after years around James, I only removed my make-up right before bed, and yet around Liam, I feel free to be unapologetically me.

He makes me feel beautiful with a simple look. My belly flutters and my phone vibrates.

Maxine: What? Oh, please tell me was he lying naked on the kitchen table covered in whipped cream...

Her message then proceeds with a couple of different GIFs. Where does she even find these? I hold the pad over my eye and then type back with my finger.

Me: No, not quite, but if I asked, I'm sure he would deliver. He got me a period care package <3

Once my face is free of makeup, I use my face wash.

You'd think at thirty I would be past breakouts, but evidently not, and even more so around the time of the month. I swear down, if I even go a day without using it, I know about it.

When I'm done, I go back to my room and add some moisturiser and run some Carmex over my lips. At least having my eyebrows and lashes tinted I don't look completely ghost like.

Maxine: O-kay, I don't know whether to be impressed or not to be honest. That boy is head over heels about you, you know that, right?

I sit on the edge of my bed. My pulse is racing, and my fingers shake a little as I reply.

Me: Don't say that! I'm just trying to not over-think this. I like him, but I don't want to hurt him either.

A sinking feeling low in my stomach has me feeling all kinds of conflicted. The thought of hurting him seriously doesn't sit well with me.

Maxine: Just enjoy whatever this is between you and be honest with him. It's all you can do. And I want all the details tomorrow.

Me: What details?

Maxine: *Aubergine emoji* and *flame emoji*

I turn my phone over in my hands as I think of the repercussions if this all goes Pete Tong.

Knuckles rap against the wood of my door and I look up to see Liam standing there, leaning against the doorjamb.

"Everything okay?" he asks, his eyes surveying my face.

Nodding, I stare down at my phone as his feet move in my peripheral vision before the bed dips and he sits beside me, his knee so close to mine I can feel the warmth of his body.

His hand comes down over mine and the phone and stills my movements.

"Hey, if we're serious about exploring this"—his index

finger moves to my chin and turns my face towards his—"then we need full transparency. Talk to me."

I bite down on my lip and can't help but smile. "When did you get so grown up?" I nudge him with my shoulder, causing him to smile in response.

"When you weren't looking."

Licking my lips, I taste the cherry flavour from my lip balm. "You want me to be honest?"

He nods and waits for me to continue.

"I'm worried that this"—I point between the two of us—"could end badly, and the last thing I'd want to do is inadvertently hurt you."

Raising my hand, my thumb strokes his short beard. "I remember the first time you and Callum shaved." The memory flashes before my eyes, they cut themselves so many times.

He laughs at that, shaking his head, tickling my palm as it brushes against his jaw.

"Yeah, we didn't even have any hair," he says, groaning.

Squeezing my thigh, his gaze holds mine. "Listen, are we taking a risk? Of course, we are, there's no certainty in life, and believe me, the thought of me hurting you isn't something I'd want even to consider a possibility. I can't give you guarantees, but I am not holding you to anything. If you want to stop this right now, I won't lie, I won't like it, but I'll accept it. I would never coerce you to be with me in any way, shape or form."

I let out an exhale of breath. His words literally give me fucking goosebumps.

My heart softens that little bit more. "I don't want to stop. I want to get to know the real you, Liam, and not just the guy I associate as my brother's best friend."

He turns his cheek and kisses the inside of my wrist. "I think I'm one and the same, but believe it or not, I want to get to know you too."

Raising my eyebrows, I let out a small chuckle. "I think you already know me plenty. I feel like I'm the one who needs to play catch up."

Surprising me in a stealthy move, he pushes me back on the bed, his torso hovering over mine. "About time, because I feel like I spent the last fifteen years trying to catch up to you, Verity Warren."

He leans closer, his tongue caressing my lips so achingly softly, teasing, silently asking for access. Who the hell am I to deny him? I part my lips and his tongue dips inside my mouth as he seeks out my tongue, and I let myself get lost in him as he kisses me with vigour. I just worry he has me on a damn pedestal, and at some point, whether I mean to or not, I'll disappoint him.

He rolls onto his back, his hands gripping my hips as he swiftly pulls me on top of him. I rest my forearms on his chest to look into his eyes.

Liam smacks his lips together before swiping his tongue over his full lower lip.

"Hmm, cherry," he says appreciatively.

Smiling, I rub mine together. "Glad you like it. You know, you're a really good kisser," I say, my fingers tracing the soft cotton of his T-shirt. I love the way it hugs his body so perfectly.

"Ditto." His head lifts and he kisses my forehead before resting his head back, his eyes scanning the ceiling.

"I always fantasied about having you here, in this room."

I feel him harden beneath me and my lower stomach stirs with excitement.

"Oh, did you now?"

He sits up so fast I let out a squeal as he holds me and moves into a standing position, lifting me with him so my feet are dangling above the ground.

"Shit, you're strong."

I don't think James ever picked me up.

"Why thank you." Liam starts walking towards the open bedroom door.

"Hey, where are we going? Didn't you just say you fantasied about having me in here with you?"

He leans in, his mouth coming down on the flesh between my shoulder and my earlobe, sucking over the bare skin, and I shiver.

"I did, but there's no rush and dinner's ready," he says into my neck, his breath so warm it sends sparks through my entire body.

Chapter Eighteen

Liam

"Oh," she says, her legs hooking around my back when she realises I have absolutely no intention of letting her go as I navigate the stairs and take her over to the dinner table, where I rest her arse just on the edge. Her legs loosen and I step back but keep myself between them.

"Well, I wouldn't have been opposed to you trying out some of these fantasies, just so you know."

My dick jerks in my pants, unsurprisingly. I've always been in a state of arousal in her presence. It was a real problem between the ages of fourteen and sixteen. It's why I was grateful for baggy tracksuits, anything that helped keep it somewhat under wraps. I can't even count the amounts of times I had to go and knock one out in their upstairs bathroom just to get it under control. But that is not something I have any intention of admitting to, not ever.

I graze the shell of her ear when I lean in to whisper my reply. "And believe me, I look forward to all the ways I dreamt of bringing you pleasure."

The hitch of her breath and the way her thighs squeeze my legs tells me she's excited to find out what that might entail, but for now, I want to ease her in slowly. As much as this chemistry is sexual, it's so much more than that.

"Later. Come on, first you need sustenance." I step back as she brings her hand to wave in front of her face.

She scoots forward and drops to her feet. "I think I like your bossy side, Liam."

I point to one of the place settings and order her to sit.

She smiles wide, her teeth on show as she slides into the chair and looks up at me.

"Good girl."

Shaking her head, she looks at the plate and then back to me, clearing her throat.

"So, Liam Carmichael, what's for dinner?" she asks, using her index finger to caress the stainless-steel fork in a way I wish she were caressing me. I turn away before I lose my self-restraint.

"Your favourite," I say and head into the kitchen.

When I return with the pan and place it between us, her eyes light up and she claps her hands together before her eyes dart to mine.

"Paella."

I nod. "Yep, dig in." Jogging back to the kitchen, I grab the warm bread rolls and the bottle of wine, and I smile when I see her scooping some onto her plate—and without even asking, she does the same for me. If I thought I was smiling before, I am pretty sure my ears will be aching later. I can't remember the last time I felt this happy.

"Wow, this smells wonderful." I love how she leans over her plate and inhales deeply.

"It's one of your favourite dishes, right?" Pouring us each a glass of wine, I hold up mine to hers and clink them together. "Cheers."

"Yep, I haven't had it in forever though."

I remember once, when she'd come back from Valencia, she wouldn't stop talking about it, so after that I asked my dad to help me make it. My mum, as much as she denies it, cannot cook for shit. He has always cooked and taken out the bins. Once, when he went away on a work trip, we had takeaway for nearly two weeks, and even I was beyond excited when he came home.

"Oh, my fucking God, Liam." Her eyes move to mine as she chews around her food. "This is delicious," she says, swallowing. She points to her plate with her fork. "Did you seriously cook this?"

I nod. "Yep. You didn't stop talking about it after you'd been to Valencia."

Her cheeks heat and she looks at me—really looks at me. "Shit, Liam, you're killing me here. I need you to start talking about yourself, and stat."

Picking up my wine, I take a small sip. I don't care for it much, but I know it's one of her favourites. She's shocked that I remember all these things, but how can I not?

"Okay, I'm going to just do a quick round of questions, no thinking too hard, just answer, okay?"

I love that she wants to know more about me, so I nod.

"Favourite colour?"

"Hazel, the colour of your eyes."

She tilts her head to the side, her fork pausing at her lips. "Are you serious?"

"Deadly. It's the colour combination of your eyes—the brown, the green and the gold."

Dropping her fork back onto the plate, she stands up and I hold my breath. Fuck, it was a matter of time before I said too much. She leans over the table and grabs hold of my T-shirt and pulls me to her, kissing me roughly before pulling back and sitting down, her nostrils flaring, her chest rising and falling underneath my hoody that makes me want to forget all about dinner and have her spread eagled before me on the table, so I can fuck her delicious cunt with my mouth. I shift in my seat. *Down boy.*

"That's really sweet." She reaches for the bread and tears off some before popping it into her mouth.

"Favourite movie?"

I work my hand through my hair.

"Pearl Harbour."

She blinks a couple of times, her breath coming out in a puff of an exhale. She's always been told she looks like Kate Beckinsale, probably why it's my favourite film. Let's just say I was intrigued it was Pearl Harbour, followed by Underworld as a very close second.

"Favourite book?"

I swallow my mouthful of food. "Interview with the Vampire."

She nods, and I swear she even looks a little impressed. "Favourite place to be?"

"Anywhere that's near a beach. I love being near water, by the ocean, in the ocean, there's nowhere better to be than immersed in water."

Dinner pretty much continues like this, she asks me a random question and I answer. When we finish eating, she goes to try to clear up the table, but I stop her and pick up our wine and walk over to the living room. She follows, placing our drinks on the coffee table, being sure to put them on coasters.

Sitting down, I pat the space next to me. "Come, sit."

She moves forward and I shake my head. "No, other end, and put your feet in my lap."

Biting her lip, she does as I ask, and I take hold of her feet, pulling them to me.

"If you tell me you have a foot fetish like my brother, we might need to just quit while we're ahead."

I throw my head back and laugh.

"You know about that?" I question.

"Yeah, he was always eyeing up my friends' feet during the

summer when they'd come round in their flip flops." She lets out an exaggerated shiver, and I smile.

"Nope, no foot fetish, just a *you* fetish," I say as my thumbs begin to knead the insole of her foot.

Verity throws her head back and lets out a soft moan, and the sound is pure fucking heaven.

Chapter Nineteen

Verity

"No, leave the flamingo alone," I mumble.

The sound of a deep laugh makes me stir as I blink my eyes open to find Liam glancing towards me, my feet still in his lap as he holds out his phone in front of him.

"Is she awake?" Callum asks, and Liam turns the phone in my direction. "Hey, Verity. What was that about a flamingo?"

I just flip him off and push myself into a seated position, crossing my legs. Shit, how did I fall asleep? I glance at the clock... and for an hour... *what the fuck?*

"Callum was just saying Boris announced a lockdown," Liam says, and I look at him and then search for the remote and switch on the TV, going straight to BBC news.

Sure enough, the headlines read a 'stay-at-home' order.

I sit forward, trying to shake the fogginess of just waking up, and hate that I was talking in my sleep in front of Liam. After he went to so much effort with dinner and that foot massage, my entire body heats, and when my eyes flick towards Liam, he has a small grin on his face.

Looking back at the TV and needing something to do with my hands and knowing my hair probably looks like a bird's nest, I pull it out of the hairband and run my fingers through it before tying it into a bun again. The entire time, I swear I can feel Liam's eyes on me as Callum chats away in the background. Pushing to my feet, I go and grab my phone. There's a message from my dad, and as expected, one from Maxine. Joining Liam back on the sofa, I tuck my legs underneath me, his hand going straight to my knee and squeezing gently.

I startle, and he goes to move his hand away, I immediately feel bad. Reaching for his hand, I place it back and see his lips curve into a smile.

He just caught me off guard is all. He's more tactile than I'm used to, but I actually quite like it. His thumb makes small circular motions, his lips curving into a content smile.

Dad: Well, looks like UK is going into lockdown. If you need anything, call Uncle Andy or one of your brothers, okay?"

I quickly reply to him first.

Me: I'll be fine, Dad, don't worry about me. I'm more concerned about you and Mum being on that cruise xx

"Is there anything you need, Verity? If you get stuck call Uncle Andy or one of the twins."

I let out a groan and lean over, leaning on Liam in the process.

"Callum, you're the baby of the family." I feel Liam tense beneath me and instantly feel bad about my remark about baby—it's only five years. "Dad already texted me saying the same thing anyway, and I'm more than capable of looking after myself."

He rolls his eyes and looks past me to get Liam's attention. "You'll make sure she's all right, won't you, man?"

Liam looks to me and nods. "Yeah, always."

I move back to the other end of the sofa, the moment feeling a little too heavy, even for me.

I pull up the other message.

Maxine: Well, it looks like we'll all be remote working after tomorrow then, meh.
Me: Why? What have you heard?
I swear they've only just announced lockdown and stay at home measures, but she already has the low down.
Maxine: Bob sent an email, which pretty much said it's going to be advised that after tomorrow we all refrain from coming in until further notice.
Me: You know he hates you calling him Bob, his name is Robert. Maybe I should login to my work email from my phone, left my laptop at work.
Maxine: I like to wind him up. Anyway, you could just unmute the work group chat.
Shaking my head, I let out a snort.
Me: Yeah, I don't think so, it gives me anxiety and I hate that Bob doesn't give a shit about talking about work at any given time of the day.
"V, Callum's going," Liam says, angling the phone in my direction again.
"Bye, love you."
"Love you too."
"Catch you later, time for me to go work my charm on Quinn."
Liam puts his phone on the table and leans his head back, closing his eyes. If anyone needed a nap earlier, I think it might have been him.
Getting up, I walk around to the back of the sofa and place my hands on his shoulders and squeeze.
He opens his eyes, looking up at me with a small smile.
"Your turn," I say. "Lay down, let me give you a massage."
He shakes his head. "No, you don't have to do that."
Leaning over the back of the sofa so I'm level with his ear, I whisper, "No, but I want to. I know my comment to Callum made you uncomfortable, and I'm sorry. So, please take off

your T-shirt and lay down so I can help you relax, like you helped me to relax."

I kiss his cheek and move around until I'm in front of him, putting my hand on my hip and raising an eyebrow.

He licks his lips and then smiles.

"Whatever you say, Verity."

Once he's settled, I climb over him and straddle his back. He lets out a deep, throaty groan.

"Is this okay?" I ask, my hands moving over his shoulders. "It would probably be better with some oils; I didn't think this through."

"No, it's perfect, your touch is indescribable."

I bite on my lower lip as I work over his shoulders and then over his back, enjoying the sounds it elicits from him, and quite frankly, arousing myself at the same time. But from the ache in my lower back and how bloated I am, my period is going to make an appearance any time now. Most of the time, I get a pounding headache right before I come on. I don't even know if that's normal. And when I think about it, it's terrible that as women we do that a lot—just accept it because we are women.

Lost in thought, I don't realise he's fallen asleep until his breathing grows heavy, and he lets out a soft snore. Wow, even his snore is handsome. Carefully, I shift myself and climb off him and head towards the kitchen with the intention of clearing up from dinner, but it's already done. I've always been a deep sleeper, but the fact he wooed me to sleep touching my feet and didn't gross me out and then did all of this too… I'm blown away.

Deciding to let him sleep, I grab the box he put together and make my way upstairs. That bath bomb has my name written all over it.

Chapter Twenty

Liam

I stretch and it takes me a minute to get my bearings. I'm still on the sofa. I reach for my phone and see it's almost one in the morning. That means I actually had five hours of sleep, uninterrupted, which is unusual for me. Verity has a special touch. She must have gone to bed because there's a throw covering me, and the only light is from the hallway.

Making my way to the kitchen, I grab myself a glass of water before making my way upstairs. There's a soft fragrance in the air, and as I approach Verity's door which is ajar, I see the self-care box I put together, and I know she's used one of the bath bombs.

Quietly, I step inside and move towards her bed. One of her bare legs is outside the cover, but I'm drawn to her deep soft breaths, and then she startles me when she starts mumbling.

"Flamingos are friends, not food."

I stifle my laugh and back away, not wanting to disturb her and have her find me in her room without an invitation.

Just as I turn to leave, I notice a printer looking thing on the desk in the corner and find myself taking a closer look.

The light from the hallway is bright enough for me to read 'Cricut Maker' along the front. What's that then?

On the desk beside it are a stack of those reusable cotton bags and I turn it over to find an inspirational quote. There's also stacks of stickers and what look like bookmarks. Someone's been busy outside of their day job.

She always was creative growing up, but whereas Callum followed his creativity, Verity thrived on the academic side of school and her career choices, but I wonder if that truly makes her happy.

It's nice to find out something new about her, even if it was by accident.

Back in Callum's room, I strip down to my boxers and pull back the covers. Even if I don't manage to get any more sleep tonight, those couple of hours definitely made up for it.

All I know is I'm desperate to explore so much more with Verity. I want to show her all the ways I feel for her and take the opportunity to do just that.

The sound of the floorboard creaking in the hallway has me looking towards the half-open bedroom door, and Verity peers inside.

"Sorry, did I wake you?" I ask, leaning on my elbows and sitting up.

She shakes her head, her eyes still sleepy as she steps into the room in a just a T-shirt and pair of shorts.

I pat the bed for her to come in and she scrunches up her nose.

And then I laugh. Yeah, it's her brother's bed.

"You want me to come to your room?" I ask.

Her smile is ridiculously cute. "Only if you want to."

I'm up and out of bed so fast she turns on her heel and rushes back to her room, with me hot on her heels.

But I grab her around the waist and pull her to my chest, holding her in place.

"I'm not sure I like you running away from me," I say in her ear.

Her back is pressed against my chest, and she turns her head and looks up, so her lips are a whisper from mine. "Not even when you're the one chasing me?" she asks, her voice still thick from just waking up.

"I'll always chase you but doesn't mean I like it."

Verity turns in my arms, her hands going to my hips. "But just think how much fun you get to have when you catch me."

I let out a groan deep from within my chest. Fucking hell, Verity really is a temptress when she's just waking up.

"When you say it like that…" I walk her backwards until her legs hit the edge of the mattress. "But you have work in the morning. Come on, bed."

Truth is, I'd happily spend all night getting fully acquainted with Verity's body and the parts I've only ever dreamed about.

"Oh, so bossy."

She climbs back on the bed and gets under the covers. I hesitate, but she pulls it back and pats the space next to her, so I get in beside her and she snuggles against me.

"Is this weird for you?"

"What? Being in a bed with you?"

I feel her move her head and I look down to find her watching me. "This and no longer being in the army. You know, I was worried about you."

My breath catches because I never thought she'd say something like that to me, but then again, she's known me practically my entire life.

"No, and not in the way I worry about Callum, not in a sisterly way, but I guess I always pushed away any thoughts that weren't purely platonic. Even then though, there's was always something underlying about you… about us."

I squeeze her shoulder and pull her closer, as if that's even possible.

"It means a lot you thought about me at all. If you knew how many times my mind wandered to you, and still does, I wouldn't blame you for locking me out of your room and putting a chair up against the handle for good measure."

She swats my chest playfully, causing my dick to twitch in my boxers. I'm just glad the duvet is hiding it and she's currently not touching me anywhere near it. Of course, I would love that, but I'll wait—I'll always wait for her.

"Well, I did, and I want you to know I did." She tries to hide her yawn, but I feel it.

I rub her back. "Come on, sleep. I don't want you falling asleep at work tomorrow and being mad at me."

Her cheek moves against my chest. "Not possible."

"Really? Do you know how many times you blasted me and Callum for keeping you up when we stayed over?"

She snuggles into me even closer. "No, but I have a feeling you're about to enlighten me."

Damn, I love her like this, so relaxed and open. I always feel like she puts on a façade, not in a fake way, but more like a protective way, and I hate it when she does.

"Every single time. Honestly, I think in the end I did it just to get some sort of reaction from you. I like to feel seen," I admit, stroking her back in slow circles, wanting so badly to feel her bare skin beneath my palm but knowing it won't stop there, not unless she asked me to anyway.

Verity moves her head and kisses my chest lightly before settling back down again.

"You were always Callum's annoying best friend."

"Tell me how you really feel," I say, laughing.

She digs her nails into me, not enough to hurt but enough to get me to shut up.

"Stop that. What I was going to say before you interrupted me is I always saw you. Yes, you've always been my kid brother's best friend, and then one day, you suddenly went from being a boy to being a man. I'm not blind, Liam, I saw you, even when I pretended I didn't."

I don't know why but I get so much satisfaction from knowing that. I say nothing in response and just enjoy holding her in the way I have always wanted to as I stare up at the glow-in-the-dark stars on the ceiling, and I fall to sleep with a smile on my face.

Chapter Twenty-One

Verity

I throw yet another work outfit on the floor and let out a frustrated sigh. Of course, the first day of the 'stay at home' order and Nick wants everyone in for a meeting and to collect anything we might need to work at home.

"For fuck's sake." I haven't come on yet but I'm starting to feel bloated.

It's already been one of those mornings, one where I wish I could climb back into bed and sleep the entire day away. Honestly, if I was alone, I probably would too, but Liam would get suspicious, and the last thing I need is him worrying about me.

Even putting on my damn makeup is a chore. I wish I had the confidence to go to work without it—I used to, and that's what irritates me the most.

"Hey, you okay?"

I look behind me to see Liam rounding the partition and coming into my walk-in wardrobe my dad built for my fourteenth birthday. I've always loved it, made me feel so grown up and special.

He leans his shoulder against the wall, frowning as he takes in the state of the floor, and most likely me.

I bend down and grab another blouse from the pile and hold it up against me and turn around and stare at my reflection in the full-length mirror.

"Yep, fine. Just having trouble finding something to wear."

He walks up behind me so we're both staring at my reflection in the mirror, only his eyes are solely focused on my face, not my bare legs or the T-shirt which happens to be the only item of clothing I'm wearing.

"Why? You always look nice," he says, pulling me against his chest and bringing me a little comfort.

I can't hide my groan. "Yeah, well, it takes a lot of time and effort to look nice," I say, using air quotes on the last word.

"Hey, what's all this about?" He rests his chin on my shoulder. When did this become so familiar and normal? I love how tactile he is with me, even when I'm feeling so bloody vulnerable.

"Nothing." I squeeze my eyes closed and inhale a deep breath.

"Don't lie to me, V." The way he says it has me opening my eyes and staring back at his reflection.

I lick my lips and exhale. "I hate the way I look, okay?"

His eyebrows shoot up and he tilts his head, his lips so close to my cheek. "Are you serious?"

He turns me and takes the blouse from me, tossing it back on the pile of clothes.

"Yeah." I feel so fucking small admitting it out loud, especially admitting it to him.

"But why?"

He takes my face in his hands and implores me to tell him, and so I do.

I clear my throat. "When I was with James, he used to comment on my appearance a lot, and when I mean comment, it was always negative, he always found something to complain about. Whether my top was too tight, too loose, my skirt too short, too long. My tights were too granny looking, or I had bare legs and therefore I was fucking around behind his back."

Liam grinds his jaw, and I notice him trying to control his breathing, but his entire body is now tense.

"Any way it doesn't matter." I go to step away, but he holds me in place.

"No, it does matter. Carry on. What else?"

I sigh loudly. "And now when I look in the mirror, all I see is every time he said something negative, every flaw he ever pointed out, and then I get so stuck in my head. His words are no longer his… now they're mine."

He nods and takes a moment as his eyes search my face, but I know he's trying to articulate a response to what I just unleashed on him.

"Turn around," he says, his voice firm but quiet, and it makes the hairs on the back of my neck stand on end.

I swallow and lick my lips. "What?"

"Please, Verity, turn around." He drops his hand from my face, and I slowly do as I'm told, and then when I'm facing the full-length mirror again, his palms come down on my shoulders and he holds me in place. I close my eyes and take a couple of deep breaths before I stare back.

"Verity, when I look at you, do you know what I see?"

I shake my head and try for a light response. "A grown woman who looks like a sack of shit."

He grits his jaw, raising an eyebrow, and I know that was not the answer he was waiting for.

"No, not even on your worst day, and I'll tell you why."

His hands move to my upper arms as he stares back at us, and I find myself holding my breath before he begins speaking again.

"I start here." He moves his hands down to mine and I watch as he takes hold of them, his touch making my insides flutter.

"Firstly, I see a beautiful woman." I almost want to sigh and pull away from him, but he cuts me off before I even get the chance.

"All the pieces that make you. You are beautiful. Like your hands." He links his fingers with mine. "These are the hands that took hold of your mum's and comforted her when you lost your grandad. As much as you were hurting, she was hurting more and you gave her strength, with everything single squeeze of your fingers." He squeezes them for emphasis and my breath catches. It's true, I was devastated. My grandad was a good man, and as heartbroken as I was, it was nothing compared to my mum. My dad and I sat either side of her on that church pew and I never let go of her hand, not once.

"I was sitting the other side of Callum; he was between us and all I wanted to do in that moment was take your other hand and comfort you."

I have to bite my lip to keep from crying, it's still so raw, thinking of that day, and even with the amount of time that's passed, it hurts. I don't think I'll ever get over his loss, but I have learned to navigate my way through it.

"And then there are your lips." He lets go of my hands and brings his to my mouth, where his thumb slowly strokes over my bottom lip, and I can't even hide my gasp as he does.

"These are the lips that have always offered words of kindness, guidance, and comfort. Even when you were at your wit's end with Callum and me, you were never cruel, Verity. Not even with any of your siblings."

He taps my temple so softly, but it sends heat through my entire body.

"And this right here, you have the most beautiful mind. And the biggest shame of all is the world doesn't even get the pleasure of seeing even one percent of just how much."

His hand slides down my throat and pauses on the top of

my chest as he pulls me tight against him, and it's hard not to ignore the way my body affects his.

Liam cocks an eyebrow and I clear my throat, amazed at how fucking well he can read me.

"Of course your body turns me on V, it's impossible not to have a physical reaction to you." And as if for emphasis, he pulls me to his erection, and I'd be lying if I said my lower stomach wasn't clenching from the action. How did I go from self-loathing only moments ago to feeling worthy and thoroughly seen?

"But it's more than your body that does this to me. Your body is the vessel, but damn, it's your soul your being that draws me in."

Chapter Twenty-Two

Liam

It's hard not to notice how the hairs on her arms rise or the way her nipples are pulled tight beneath her flimsy fucking T-shirt, but this is more about her soul and what I see beneath the surface than it is about her appearance, and I just want her to see what I do when I look at her—when I really look at her.

I bring my palm down and slightly to the left just over her breasts, and her breath hitches in a way I find mesmerising.

"But this right here," I say, holding her gaze with mine, hoping to convey more than just words. "Your heart, the way you love and have the ability to care for others, even when they don't deserve it, that's what I see. All your body parts are just extensions of you. How you listen to others, how you talk to them, how you care for them."

Her eyes are glistening with unshed tears, as her heart races beneath my palm.

"Wow." She lets out a breath. "And you see all of that when you look at me?"

I lean closer to her ear, and whisper, "I see more than there are words or letters in the alphabet to describe what I see. But yes, I see that and so much more."

She turns now and wraps her arms around me, pressing her ear to my chest as I hold her.

"Thank you," she says and then looks up, her eyes dancing all over my face.

"You don't have to thank me; you just have to start counteracting every bad thought and comment that arsehole ever threw your way. I won't lie though, Verity, I'm not a violent man, but if I was ever alone in a room with him, my fists would probably do the talking."

And it's the truth. I have never wanted to hit somebody as much as I do him right now, and I know if Callum even had a small idea of just how bad he treated her mentally and emotionally, he would probably castrate the fucker.

"I wouldn't ever want you to stoop that low, he's not worth it, but you are, Liam Carmichael. And yes, I do need to thank you for being you in every way that matters. All the times you've done things for me without me even knowing."

I lean down and kiss the tip of her nose, and she gives me a genuine smile.

"Do you know, when you kissed me the first time—or when I kissed you"—I laugh and nod, because yeah, she did initiate that—"I felt like that was my first real kiss, and it was someone I didn't even know. I felt so many things, and even though I was in an 'off stage' with James, I still felt like I'd been the one in the wrong. Even then, he had a way of manipulating me, and yet, I just went along for the ride."

Bending down, I lower my face so our lips are inches apart.

"Let me show you and remind you for as long as you'll allow me at how truly remarkable you are. I want to see you believe it again too."

"Okay," she says.

"Okay," I reply, just as her lips meet mine for a tender kiss, and I don't know what it is but there is something different in this kiss, something that's never been there before, and if I could bottle this feeling and save it for those rainy days, fuck me, I would.

"I really should get ready for work," she says, pulling out of the kiss and grabbing whatever clothes her fingers land on. "Are you going to watch me dress?" she asks playfully, the heaviness of the situation abating a little.

"Not if you want me to leave."

Giving her control, I wait for her to answer, and instead she shocks the hell out of me when she drops the clothes back on the pile, reaches down and pulls the T-shirt up and over her head, standing before me in only a pink lacy thong—pink might just be my new favourite colour.

Her cheeks heat and I see her fingers tremble, but I know she needs this if she's ever going to find her true confidence again. I trail my eyes to hers and suck in a breath with the wanton look in her eyes.

"How long do you have before you need to be out the door to leave?" I ask.

She glances to her watch. "I have to leave in twenty minutes."

I take a step forward, her nipples hard. "How about you let me take care of you, give you something to think about while you're there?"

Dropping to my knees before her, I look up, waiting for her to answer. I love the way her chest rises and falls with every intake and exhale of breath.

The small nod of her head is all I need before I dip my fingers underneath the material of her thong and slide it down her legs, lifting each foot for her to step out of them before I bring them to my face and inhale, all while maintaining eye contact. I love how her skin flushes.

"I'll be keeping these," I say and stuff them into my pocket.

I reach for her calve and lift her leg over my shoulder, and she automatically reaches out to steady herself with her hand on my other one.

Kissing up the inside of her thigh, she lets out a heavy breath and I hear the moment she holds her breath when I reach her centre, and I pause, waiting an excruciating few seconds before the tip of my tongue circles her clit.

"Oh my God," she hisses through her teeth. "I can't believe I'm letting you do this in the light of day too," she says.

"I can stop," I reply, pulling back and looking up into her dark eyes.

"Don't you dare." Her fingers tug on my hair, directing me back to where she wants me, and I can't hide my chuckle.

I lick the length of her before spearing her with my tongue, and she arches into me.

"Liam…" She sighs.

As much as I could lick her out for an eternity, I know she still needs to get ready and leave. It helps she's wet and ready, so bringing my fingers to her entrance, I insert two and her hot channel clamps around them as I fuck her with my fingers, and again the thought of my dick having that honour causes me to grow painfully hard in my joggers, but that can wait. Right now, all I want to do is have her screaming my name around my tongue and fingers until she comes all over them.

Chapter Twenty-Three

Verity

I have no idea how I'm even holding myself upright as he continues with his ministrations. The way he is working me with his tongue and fingers is making me greedy for so much more, but I am too consumed by the build-up. My fingers tug at his short hair in a tight vice like grip, urging him to go deeper, faster, slower, fuck, whatever it is I need him to do, he needs no instruction from me because he's doing it already.

"Oh my God, Liam." He makes me want to scream his name until the neighbours hear me in the height of pleasure.

I swear, a cross between a groan and a growl vibrates through my clit, and it's the trigger that has me coming all over his fingers and his tongue. It's unyielding and relentless, just the stress reliever I didn't even know I needed.

He continues until my orgasm begins to subside with light pulsing and aftershocks. He kisses my stomach before resting my other leg on the ground and rising to his full height.

And before I even have a chance to catch my breath, his lips are on mine. And I love how I taste on his tongue and his lips. Ending the kiss, he pulls me against his chest for a moment, and I rest my hand on his chest to feel his heart racing beneath my palm.

"That was... amazing, thank you," I say, my face now buried against his chest, burning with heat.

"Do you feel better?" he asks, his voice deep but sated.

"I do." I wish I could stand with him like this all day and not let go, but adulting waits for no one.

Reluctantly, I pull back and he leans down and kisses my forehead. Snatching up my clothes and getting a fresh thong from my underwear drawer, I walk out of the walk-in wardrobe and walk through my room and across to the bathroom, leaving Liam in my room as I go to dress.

He's sitting at my desk when I come back in my room, and I pause when I see him looking at the designs I created the other night. Glancing up, he smiles when I approach him, turning in the swivel chair and pulling me between his legs.

"Stunning," he says, but I swear his eyes never once left my face when he looked up, and I kind of like that.

"So, are you going to share this titbit about yourself you've been keeping secret?" he asks, reaching for one of my designs.

"Not really a secret, just something I started doing in my spare time," I admit.

"Well, it's good, V, really good. You should sell them."

Stepping out of his touch, I take it from him and place it back on the desk and worry my bottom lip.

"Yeah, maybe."

I'm not brave like Callum, but I really wish I was.

"Don't. Don't do that, V." Liam gets to his feet and cups my face in his hands. "You are just as capable as anyone else. If you want to pursue your passion, fucking pursue it."

The way he is so damn passionate about telling me to follow my passion is admirable.

"God, are you even real? You know you're too good to be true, right?" And the prospect of whatever this is ending hits me hard, which is ridiculous because we've barely begun. And yet, I already know if I let myself, I will fall so deep that I'll never find my way out again.

The thought of losing him when the reality of the situation comes to light hits me hard in the gut.

"I'll let you get to work. But if you need anything, text me, okay?"

I nod. He's so damn thoughtful.

"Come on, the sooner you get to work, the sooner you can come home."

I drive to work in a daze and barely remember getting out of the car. It's only when I'm intercepted by Maxine that I come back to reality.

"Somebody got lucky," she says, wiggling her eyebrows and holding out a cup of coffee.

"A lady never tells," I say, taking the cup from her. "Thank you."

"Well, how else am I going to live my life vicariously through you if you keep it all to yourself?"

God, I love this girl.

"Anyway, you'll have to keep me posted via messages now we all have to stay at home."

The prospect of working from home and seeing Liam throughout the day fills my belly with butterflies. I can't remember the last time I was actually excited about something.

I internally cringe. We're going into lockdown and all I can think about is Liam.

"What has you thinking so hard?" Maxine asks as we all make our way into the boardroom for a meeting.

"Just that… I won't lie, being with Liam twenty-four seven fills me with equal parts excitement and apprehension."

We both pull out one of the board room chairs, which are a little over the top in my humble opinion, but whatever.

"Man, if I was stuck in lockdown with him, I assure you, I'd be getting absolutely zero work done. Zilch. I'd be too busy orgasming."

On her last word, the room goes silent and she just shrugs, and it would appear I'm the one blushing enough for the two of us. This girl gives zero fucks, and I wish I had half her confidence.

"Okay, so everyone will be working from home as of today and for the foreseeable future, at least until restrictions are eased."

Maxine rolls her eyes and I hide behind my coffee, knowing exactly what she's already thinking.

"Your time online will be monitored, so if anyone thinks this is a free pass, you're sorely mistaken."

My phone vibrates and I quickly retrieve it in case it's my parents with an update about their situation.

I'm unable to hide my smile when I see who it's from.

Liam: You are strong, and you are beautiful.

Maxine leans over, not too subtly, as she reads over my shoulder. I try to pull it away, but it's no use.

"Man, I want him. Please let me have him. Can I please?" she asks, and at least she whispers that part.

I try to stifle my laugh as I shake my head. "I already licked him, so he's mine."

She shakes her head and pokes out her tongue. "Ever heard of sharing?"

"Sorry, Maxine, can you pay attention, this is serious," says Nick, the manager who always seems to have a stick up his arse.

Crossing her arms, she plasters on a serious expression. "Apologies, please continue."

There is definitely something underlying between these two. She glances to me, and I raise my eyebrows.

"What?" she mouths.

I shake my head and point towards Nick and mouth back, "Pay attention."

Once the meeting is over, Nick asks to speak to Maxine, and I try to act like I'm not stalling for time before I reluctantly leave and go to my office to retrieve my laptop and my folders.

Just as I'm closing my door, Maxine comes out of the boardroom, looking red in the face.

"Everything okay?" I ask.

She shakes her head. "He's such a sourpuss," she says, tucking her arm into mine and walking back through to the main reception.

"Non-essential contact," Nick says as he passes us by.

She flips him off behind his back.

"Okay, seriously, what the fuck?"

Pulling me in for a quick hug, she squeezes and then lets me go. "You don't want to know."

I raise my eyebrows. "Fine, I'll message you," she says, looking around. "Anyway, be safe, text me, and I'll see you on the flip side."

Chapter Twenty-Four

Verity

We've been playing this game back and forth for days, and I know why he's held back. We've kissed, fooled around, but we're yet to have sex, and it's as though he's been waiting for me to give him the go ahead. I won't lie, the build-up to this very moment has been electrifying.

I could kiss him for an eternity and never get bored. The way he says so much without saying a single word. The way he makes me feel alive with every touch and brush of our hands, the linking of our fingers, and the way he lets me cuddle up to him on the sofa when we watch TV. How he covers me with a blanket when he notices the hairs on my arms are on end. I don't tell him that's a reaction to being so close to him.

But tonight is about to change. I want him, in a way I've never wanted anyone before.

He sits on the sofa, ready to settle in for a film, the only light coming from the television, reminding me of the night I caught him watching porn and wanking himself off. My nipples grow hard, and my hand moves to his crotch, where he's already hard beneath my palm.

I wonder if he's been hard around me this past week.

"V?" His forehead rises to his hairline as I deftly pop the top button of his jeans, the tip of his shaft already peeking out of the waistband.

His hand comes down over the top of mine, holding me there, but then as I move against him, his hand pushes down on mine, urging me on as he tilts his head back, his lips part, his eyes closed as I lower his zip. At the sound, his head lulls forward and he watches my hand. Needing better access, I move in front of him and drop to my knees. I pull the waistband of his jeans and boxers lower, and he lifts his arse as I drag them down to his thighs and over his knees, tugging them off at the ankles and tossing them away from me.

I look up and his jaw is set in a hard line, which is even more prominent with his beard. His nostrils flare and his eyes look almost black from where I am.

Taking his erection in my hand, I slowly work my way up and down before letting go and licking my palm.

"Fuck."

Bringing it back to his shaft, I lick the other, taking him in both hands.

"Shit, V." I can't hide my smirk. I learnt this in a google search when I was trying to spice up my sex life with James—hell, I even bought a vast selection of toys, toys that never even saw the light of day.

But now I'm wondering if I could put them to use.

Twisting my wrists, I know I'm working him into a frenzy from the way his fists are clinched beside him and the rise and fall of his chest as his breathing picks up.

"Do you want a little porn for some background noise?" I ask, and his eyes spring open as he stares at me and shakes his head.

"Fuck, as much as I would be down for that any other time, tonight, I just want it to be the two of us."

My belly flutters from his answer and I lean forward, and using the tip of my tongue, I swirl it in small circles over his engorged head while I simultaneously work him with my hands.

A loud hiss escapes him as he thrusts closer, entering my mouth.

"You're killing me," he says, his voice cracking slightly on the last word.

My fingers move to his balls as I cup them and play with them as I take him to the back of my throat, enjoying how he tastes.

"Stop," he grunts, and I can't help but laugh as he gently pushes me away and moves me to my feet.

With a mastered technique, he reaches over the back of his head and whips his T-shirt off, and my eyes go wide. I move back and switch on the lamp, not taking my eyes off him when I move closer, my fingers tracing over his abs and sides. He turns, and I notice a mark and spin him to get a closer look as his hand covers mine.

I look up and he shakes his head once.

"You don't want to talk about it?"

"Not tonight."

Nodding in understanding, I remove his hand from mine and then kiss him over the bumpy scars before moving back to his chest and tracing my tongue from his chest to his abs.

His smell is so uniquely him, it's intoxicating, the most enticing masculine scent. How did I never notice it before?

"My turn," he says, pinning my arms to my sides to stop me from touching him as he brings his lips down to mine, kissing me so I feel it in my toes.

When we come up for air, he spins me, so my back is flush against his chest. His hand moves up and underneath the off-the-shoulder lounge top I'm wearing as his finger dips under the waistband of my joggers. Teasing my skin, he leaves soft kisses on my shoulder and clavicle before taking my earlobe in his mouth. I arch into his erection.

"Easy, baby." Fucking hell, him calling me baby is hot.

"Up."

I lift my arms above my head as he pulls my top off and spins me to face him, as his eyes rake over my lacy black bra. He pings one of the straps. "Did you wear this for me?"

His eyes are glazed over, full of lust.

Swallowing, I try to keep my voice even, wanting to be every bit as confident as I've been imagining these past few days.

"I did, I have the matching thong too."

Instantly, he drops to his knees with a loud thud, his fingers pulling at the waistband of my joggers and slowly dragging them down to my feet, where he lifts one of my feet followed by the other until they are discarded with his clothes.

Leaning close, he takes a huge intake of breath, and I know he's smelling me just as I was smelling him.

"Am I going to find your sweet pussy wet and wanting?"

Before I can form a response, his lips come down and suck over the material, and I jerk into him. My fingers gravitate to his head, and I grab a fistful of his hair. God, everything with him is a sensory overload, even his hair feels fucking fantastic.

When he pulls back, he looks up at me through hooded eyes.

"I'm going to need these off." And just when I think he can't surprise me anymore, he reaches out and rips them off me in one go. My hands go to his shoulders to keep me from slamming into him.

Damn, that was fucking hot, and if I had any doubt about him being a boy, I was truly fucking mistaken. I want to scold him, tell him I love that set, but I don't get the chance as he stands to his full height and wraps his arm behind my back, and with the flick of his thumb and forefinger, my bra comes down.

"Okay, I'm torn between being impressed and jealous." The thought of him using those same techniques on other women makes me want to give him a show he won't forget.

He backs me up, my calves hitting the sofa, and I move to lay down, the leather cool beneath my skin as he crawls over me. Any thoughts I had about taking control dissipate when his strong, calloused palms spread my thighs. I'm literal putty in his hands as his finger traces my clit before slipping inside me, and I let out a small cry of ecstasy.

Chapter Twenty-Five

Liam

"Is this what you want, V? You want to me to sink my cock into your wet and aching core?"

My eyes roam up the length of her body. She nods and bites down on her lip, her fingers playing with her puckered nipple.

I continue to fuck her with two fingers and then add a third for emphasis.

"Ahh, yes, Liam, that feels…" Her words trail off when I begin to circle her clit with my tongue, and she bucks at the contact. When I suck her into my mouth, she lets out a mewling sound, which only adds to my own arousal.

I'm in a purgatory state, stuck between heaven and hell, wanting to take my time devouring her before we finally join as one, but also wanting so desperately to claim her in the most animalistic way.

Our first time together shouldn't be rushed, I want to cherish every inch of her flesh and bring her to the brink, only to ease off so that when she does finally come, it's with me buried so deep inside her she doesn't know where she begins or I end.

Even if this isn't the same for her as it is for me, I want this to be a core memory, something she'll never be able to forget, whether she's with me or not.

I want to hear her beg me for release, scream out my name while I fuck her into oblivion.

Her walls start to clench around my fingers, and I know she's close, so I withdraw them completely. I bring them up to my mouth and suck them, licking off her sweet, sultry taste.

She sits up on her elbows and cuts her eyes in my direction, and I can't help but chuckle.

"I swear to God, Liam, you better make me come soon or I'm going to finish the job myself."

The thought of me watching as she gives herself an orgasm is actually one I could get behind, but it sure as hell will not be today.

"So impatient," I tease.

She throws her head back in frustration.

"You're testing my patience," she says. And fuck me if I don't enjoy watching her coiled up tight like this—all the better when I do finally give her what we both desperately crave.

"The only one who will be making you come tonight is me. And if I have to tie you down to prove my point, believe me, I will." I spread her folds with my fingers, teasing her slit.

And when I look at her face, her lips part as she lets out a ragged breath, her tongue sweeping over her swollen bottom lip. Her pupils dilate and her nostrils flare ever so softly.

"You wouldn't," she says, but it sounds more like a question or a dare, and from the way she's squirming, it has me thinking she'd enjoy just that.

"I would, I don't ever say things I don't mean, Verity."

She visibly swallows, her eyes darting from my face to her pussy as I continue to tease her entrance.

"Then make me fucking come already," she grits out. "Or I promise you, I *will* do it myself," she says again, and this time, it's a challenge.

Making a tsking sound, I let my hand fall away and push to my feet, hovering over her.

"Don't say I didn't warn you."

Just looking at her while touching myself is enough to make me lose my shit, but I hold fast, loving the way her eyes barely even blink as she watches me with rapt attention that shuts my feisty little temptress up.

"You see what you do to me?"

My thumb smears over the pre-cum dripping from my engorged head as I lean closer—she's panting now.

Gripping my base with my other hand, I bring my thumb to her mouth, and without instruction, she sucks it into her mouth and swirls her tongue over it before biting down gently and groaning.

When she releases it, I lean down and take her mouth in mine and kiss her. It's not gentle or sweet, it's demanding and full of fire and a glimpse at what's to come.

"Please," she pleads when I pull back, and I can't help but smile.

Something about Verity Warren begging me to take her is my undoing. I kneel between her legs and stroke my dick over her wet pussy.

Her legs wrap around my hips and pull me closer to her core.

"I fucking love how much you want me," I say, licking her clavicle with a slow, torturous swipe of my tongue. She pulls me closer, my tip just in her entrance, and I know in this very moment I am done for as I thrust into her bottoming out.

"Fuck," we both call out at the same time.

I stay where I am for a moment, the glory of me filling and stretching her is far beyond what my imagination could have ever conjured.

"Condom," I hiss through my teeth and begin to pull out. Her legs squeeze me harder, the heels of her feet pushing against my bare arse.

"No, don't, I have an IUD and I was tested after me and Ja—" I lean over and kiss her lips, not wanting her to say another man's name, not when I'm the one inside her. I pull back and nod in understanding, she doesn't need to say anymore.

I drive back into her, and her body moves from the force and then I roll my hips.

"Oh shit," she says, breathless. "Yes, just like that."

"I wanted to go slow." Long thrust. "Bring you to the brink of pleasure, over and over again." Deep thrust. "But you drive me so fucking wild." Hard thrust. "I just want more, to be closer, deeper." I ease all the way out and then back with a long, slow thrust.

Verity's eyes flutter open as she stares up at me, her soul completely bare to mine in this moment, and the sight physically takes my breath away.

"We have time for that later, but for now just do it, Liam. Take what you need and give me what I want."

I grab a cushion and stuff it under her lower back so it changes the angle, as I grip her hips hard enough to leave marks, but she doesn't seem bothered as her nails scrape down my back with a slight sting.

And so, I do exactly what she demands; I fuck her relentlessly, her walls fluttering around my dick as it turns into a steel rod, my balls tightening.

Letting go of one of her hips, I reach down and circle her clit. If I wasn't so determined to be the only one to make her come, I'd have told her to touch herself, but not today—today I will own every fucking second of her orgasm.

Chapter Twenty-Six

Verity

"Fucking hell, V, you're killing me," Liam hisses through his clenched teeth as he drives into me over and over again, his thumb working my clit in the most intoxicating way.

The way he keeps hitting me deep inside is sending me over the edge.

"V, you need to fucking come for me," he grunts out between thrusts as he hits my G-spot.

"Oh my God." I arch into him, practically levitating at this point. Something profound builds, I feel so full like I'm about to wet myself, but I'm too consumed with all the sensations vying for my attention.

And then I think I'm about to self-combust as I come so hard, spraying him. He lets out a groan which is closer to a growl deep from within his chest.

"That's it, baby, you're fucking soaking me."

He continues to fuck me through my orgasm. At this point, he's the puppet master and I am completely at his mercy. I've never experienced a release like this, it's the most exhilarating experience I've ever had; I can't even begin to describe it.

Unexpected Love

Liam tenses above me, throwing his head back as he comes in thick, hot bursts, filling me with his release.

He falls on top of me a little haphazardly, still buried inside me, before rolling us so we're on our sides, our breathing still erratic.

My hair is sticking to the back of my neck when he pulls out of me with a slick, wet sound.

Now I'm coming down from the euphoria of mere minutes ago, it hits me how I lost control of myself, and I lower my face and squeeze my eyes closed.

"Hey, V, look at me." He tilts my chin until we're eye level. "What's wrong?"

I stutter as I try to reply and pull my chin out of his grasp and sit up, reaching for his discarded T-shirt as I try to cover myself up.

"Please don't fucking try to hide from me, not after that."

I glance back and see the hurt in his eyes, and instantly, I feel guilty.

"It's not that, it's just I made a mess. Nothing like that has ever happened to me before."

He sits forward and grips the back of my neck, holding me in place.

"Good, and if you're embarrassed, don't be. It was fucking hot, Verity. I love that you drenched me with your cum."

I bite my lip, preening at his compliment, and love how vulgar he sounds—it's hot as hell too.

"It's just overwhelming this, us," I say, pointing between us.

His eyes sparkle like he knows something I don't, his lips curving into the most devilish smile. "To you maybe, but for me, I've been dreaming of being with you like this. And it was even better than my imagination could ever have dreamed up."

My skin heats from his words and I don't even have a response to that. He kisses the tip of my nose and somehow that gesture feels deeper than what we just shared. My heart beats wildly in my chest.

"Stay here, I'll get you a cloth and clean this up," he says.

He gets to his feet, his semi hard erection bobbing up and down until he turns and I get the perfect view of his arse cheeks.

I'm torn between using his top to clean between my legs or clean up the sofa and then go get the antibacterial spray and a cloth, but it's not something I need to worry about when Liam returns with a flannel in his hand and a couple of towels.

Without asking, he kneels before me. "Up," he says in a low timber voice.

I stand, his come and mine running down my thighs. He puts a towel on the wet spot that was beneath me before he takes his time cleaning me up with the warm flannel and then patting me dry with a small towel.

He looks up at me through hooded lids before leaning forward and kissing my stomach softly, and then he moves to his feet.

Taking my hand, he says nothing as he leads me upstairs and into the bathroom. He only let's go to turn on the shower. Checking the temperature, he pulls me in with him and guides me under the shower head.

Silently, he dips my head back and wets my hair before reaching for the shampoo and working it into a lather. I let out a contented sigh, everything he does is so damn intimate.

Once he's rinsed my hair and conditioned the ends before rinsing it again, I turn to face him, wrap my arms around him and lean my cheek against his chest.

He doesn't say anything, just rubs soothing circles over my back.

How is it he's managed to make me feel cherished in only a few hours, and yet, I never felt like I was good enough for James? And then, before I can stop myself, tears begin to fall and I'm a blubbering mess.

Liam's arms tighten around me before his hands move to my arse and he lifts me up, so I have no choice but to wrap my legs around him. He's hard between us, but the way he's looking at my face tells me that's not what he's concerned about right now.

"It's okay, V. I got you," he says quietly.

I lean my face towards his and kiss him. My tears mix with the shower water as he kisses me back. It's as though he's trying to say all the things he can't with his kiss.

Pulling back, he backs me against the wall and rests his forehead against mine.

He keeps me where I am, with one arm underneath my arse as the other comes up to cup my face, his thumb wiping under my eyes. I let out a small shiver.

"Come on, let's get cleaned up and get you out of the shower before you start getting cold."

My heart squeezes. He's always been very considerate, but having him all to myself like this and me being the centre of his affection is something to behold. He's so attentive with me, and other than my parents, nobody has ever treated me with such devotion.

I nod and he lowers me to my feet as he reaches for my shower gel, his intention clear, so I reach for his and we work around one another's hands as we wash each other thoroughly. When we're done, he turns off the shower and drapes me in a huge bath towel before handing me a smaller one for my hair and grabbing one for himself.

Tipping my head upside down, I wrap my hair in the towel, and when I flick my head back, he's watching me, his movements temporarily frozen before he carries on drying himself off.

Is it weird how much I love the quiet that comes with being in his presence? There's no pretence or forced conversations, and it's quite liberating. I feel free to be unapologetically myself.

Chapter Twenty-Seven

Liam

Laying with her in my arms, I don't think I have ever felt so content. Her soft breaths are like a homing beacon, one that calls to my soul.

I know the moment she stirs, and I brush my hand over her lower back.

"What time is it?" she mumbles against my chest before pressing a light kiss just over my heart.

"It's still early, baby, you go back to sleep."

She shifts and looks up at me. "But you're awake." Her hand comes up and gently cups my cheek.

"I'm good."

I love seeing her like this, just the two of us, alone, together.

"Well, I don't like that you're lying there awake, bored, while I'm using you as a giant cushion." My other hand resting on her bare thigh squeezes, before sliding around to the leg thrown over mine as I gently trail up her bed shorts and to her core.

"What makes you think I'm bored?" I tease.

She moves into my touch and a low moan escapes me.

"Believe me, if you were touching me there is no way I'd sleep through it."

I smile. "Now there's a challenge. Imagine waking up just as your climax was cresting."

Her giggle vibrates through my torso, but I also don't miss the way she moves closer to my touch.

"Why, is that something you'd like to wake up to? Are you hinting at what you'd like me to do to you?"

"Anything you do to me, I already more than like. But I'm not impervious to waking with your mouth wrapped around my cock."

"Oh, is that so?" I feel her hand slide over my groin before making contact with my dick, which of course is already semi hard. Not a difficult feat with her body against mine.

She grips me in a fist, and then in an expert move works the length of me a few times before moving lower, her intention clear.

"Hey, you don't have to do—" I'm abruptly cut off when her lips wrap around the head of my shaft, her tongue lapping up the pre-cum, and I instantly grow harder. "Fuck."

"Hmm-hmm." She hums around me, and she takes me deep to the back of her throat. I thrust up from the action and throw the cover off us and reach over to the lamp, desperate to watch. We both blink from the shock of the light, but she remains firmly in place as she cups my balls one at a time, increasing the pleasure flowing through my entire body.

Verity looks up through hooded lids as I get lost in a sublime sensory adventure as she drags my length out of her mouth, her teeth gently grazing the underside of my arousal. I want to throw my head back and close my eyes, but I don't want to miss a second of this either.

"Fucking hell, V, I could get used to this."

Every so often, her tongue glides along my shaft, gently applying pressure, and then she'll switch it up and trace the head—it's enough to drive me completely wild, especially with her sounds of pleasure vibrating through me too.

She takes me deep to the back of her throat again and she gags but quickly recovers. Her movements speed up and my hand moves to the crown of her head, but instead of taking control like the beast in me wants to, I grip her hair between my fingers. Just as I think I'm on the verge of crossing over to the point of no return, she slows down, and it's impossible not to savour every fucking caress of her lips, her tongue, and her mouth.

The way she's devouring me with such desperation, like she's never tasted something so good, makes me want to bang on my chest in triumph and holler, 'I am the man.'

But she's killing me. It's getting to the point I'm uncomfortably aroused the more she explores every fucking inch of me. And if there was any concern she wasn't enjoying it, I need not worry, because every moan that passes her lips and the way she grins around my cock is clear she's just as turned on as I am.

"Shit, V, I'm so fucking close, but I want to be balls deep inside you when I come."

Slowly, excruciating slowly, she eases off me. The tip of her tongue swirls around my head once, and then she sits up, her eyes dark with desire, her hair a mess and her chin wet from sucking me off.

"How do you want me?" she asks as she gets to her feet, the mattress dipping as she puts one hand on the wall to steady herself and shimmies out of her shorts.

"Fuck. I want you to stand over me so I can see how wet your cunt is for me."

Her confidence is exhilarating, as she does exactly that with no hesitation.

My hands run up the back of her calves and squeeze.

"Sit on my face, now."

She doesn't answer, just spreads her legs that bit more and

positions her knees either side of my head and then lowers herself towards my face, hovering.

I reach up and massage her arse cheeks as I position her right where I want her before flicking out my tongue and then swiping her from back to front in a long motion.

"Shit," she hisses from above, her hands flat against the wall.

The good thing about this being her childhood room is it's not that big. We're in a small double bed in the corner of the room, which means you can only get in and out on one side of the bed or climb off at the end.

"Don't hover, sit on my face and fuck me with that wet as sin pussy. Show me how much you enjoyed sucking my cock."

Her body quivers. She's not used to me talking dirty to her, but I know she loves it just from her body language alone.

Never one to disappoint, she sinks onto my face with some of her weight bearing down on me as I begin to fuck her with my mouth.

I make it a point to change the pace, speeding up and slowing down, pulling my tongue out, licking up the length of her, knowing I'm driving her just as wild as she drove me.

Her walls begin to flutter around my tongue, and not being one to deny her even an ounce of pleasure, I reach up and circle her clit as she comes all over my face, pulsing around me, body shuddering as she lets out a guttural moan.

Moving my hands to her hips, I lift her off my face and don't even need to tell her what I want. Her hand reaches out between us until she has me in a firm grip, aligning herself with her entrance, and then I push my hips up and thrust inside her as she sinks until I'm sheathed to the hilt.

Chapter Twenty-Eight

Verity

I barely come down from the intense orgasm and I'm covering his dick as he thrusts up inside me. My channel is still pulsing from the aftershocks. He sits forward, his abs so defined by the movement and covered in a sheen of sweat.

"Wrap your legs around me," he instructs, and I do, and I'm so fucking full now as he moves to the edge of the bed. "You want to be the one to fuck me, baby?"

I nod my head as Liam moves his hand between us and artfully stimulates my clit, keeping his eyes focused on me the entire time. The moment is so fucking intimate, it makes my chest ache as I move up and down his length.

No one has ever looked at me or worshipped me the way he does.

When he moves his hands to my hips and begins to control the thrusts, I lean back and rest my hands on his knees. Undulating my hips, the more he thrusts, the more out of control I feel. I bring my hands to his shoulders and then wrap my arms around his neck, my front flush with his, my clit rubbing up against him in the most torturous way.

His head dips as he takes a nipple into his mouth and bites

down just enough for it to cause me pain, but in the most delicious way, before doing the same to the other.

I try to hold off as long as I can, but it's impossible, I feel my orgasm cresting as my body tenses. My toes coil tight and I start coming around him, all over him.

"Fuck, Liam," I cry out as I try to catch my breath. He keeps thrusting up beneath me, his dick swelling impossibly harder, and then he comes with a low guttural moan as my name passes his lips like a sacred prayer.

His heart beats against my chest, matching my own, and when I pull back to look at his face, my breath catches all over again, before his lips take mine in a kiss that will forever be seared into my memory.

Part of me feels like crying because I know whatever happens I'm not coming out of this the same person as I went in. Whether I meant for it to happen or not, it's out of my control, and I know Liam will always own a part of me, in a way no other ever has or ever will.

I collapse on top of him, both of our bodies moving together as one with the rhythm of our breathing.

When I wake up, I'm in bed alone. The space where Liam should be is cold. I don't even remember him pulling out of me last night or this morning, or whenever it was. I stretch my arms above my head and let out a yawn, loving how my body feels after being with Liam. I get out of bed and love that feeling between my legs as I pull on a T-shirt and then go relieve myself. I hear my phone and go back in my room and bring up my WhatsApp group chat 'Terrible Trio'.

Ali: Autumn just cut her first tooth. *picture of a very tired momma and her second born*

Sarah: I don't know how you do it, I can't even potty train the dog.

Sarah was married two… three years ago, and she and her husband, Jeff, both took a sabbatical and went travelling for six months before coming back and getting a Great Dane.

Ali: On a wing and a prayer at this point.

Me: Well, I never thought I'd be back at my parents' house and in my childhood bedroom, that's for sure.

I take a quick photo of my room and send it over.

Sarah: But you're happier now, aren't you? James was never good enough for you.

Me: I am happier <3

Ali: Good, life is too short, Verity.

I love that I never lost touch with them, and as much as James would have been delighted if I had, it would have just been something else he took from me. I was lucky that no matter what they always showed up.

Sarah and Jeff even offered for me to stay with them, but with them living in Chelmsford, the commute to and from work would have been too much even for me. Besides, it's kind of been nostalgic coming back to my parents' for a bit anyway.

"Good morning, V."

I smile as Liam enters the room with a mug in each hand, and I push myself up into a seated position. He puts the cups on the bedside table and then picks one back up by the middle so I can take the handle. It's not lost on me how he did that so I wouldn't burn myself, and it's gestures like that which make my insides come alive.

"Thank you."

He kisses my forehead and then sits beside me, reaching for his tea.

"What time did you get up?" I ask, before taking a sip of mine.

"About an hour ago."

His free hand goes to my thigh and rests there, like his touch has always belonged to me.

"You should have woken me."

"Nah, I like watching you sleep."

I turn my face so I can see his, and I realise he's not joking either.

"You watched me sleeping?"

He smirks when he looks back at me and nods.

Part of me feels a little embarrassed, and the other part feels strangely content in the knowledge.

"How are you feeling after last night? Any regrets?"

I look over to gauge his facial expression and seeing him uncertain and vulnerable makes my heart ache.

"I feel good, better than good. What about you? Do you have any regrets? Isn't there some saying about when you finally get something you've wanted?"

He takes my cup from me and places it on the bedside table, and then he pulls me across his lap.

"I promise I will never regret anything with you, not ever."

"Good to know. And how do *you* feel?" I ask, wiggling my eyebrows.

Suddenly, the air leaves my lungs and I'm on my back, his weight bearing down on me, pushing me into the mattress as he rises on his elbows, caging me in.

"I feel like I will never get enough of exploring your delectable body."

I can feel his arousal between us and heat fuels deep in my belly, lighting every nerve ending in my body. Then his tongue darts out, tasting my skin as his lips trail a scorching path to the hollow of my throat.

Just as I'm getting lost in the sensation, the doorbell rings.

He groans and pushes himself off me.

"Who the hell is that?"

"I ordered us breakfast. Didn't expect it to arrive so fast."

Liam moves to get off the bed, but I stop him when I grab his wrist.

"Thank you."

He leans back over me, sucks my bottom lip between his and then pulls back. "Hold that thought, V. Once you've eaten, I plan on working up your appetite again."

Chapter Twenty-Nine

Liam

As much as I want to spend the entire weekend fucking her senseless, I'm also not a complete arsehole.

"Did you have anything you needed to do today?" I ask.

Her fingers play with the dusting of chest hair until they stray to my scar over my right side.

"Just a little bit of work on the Cricut later, but I'm good for now. Unless you have somewhere else you need to be?"

I reach down and tug her up until she's level with my face.

"I want to be wherever you are."

Her eyes soften and I love how the gold flecks of the hazel are prominent when she's looking at me like that.

I can still feel her fingers tracing the shape of my scar, and it causes me to let out a small shudder and her hand stills.

"Shit, sorry, does it hurt?" Her eyes glance down and then back to my face.

"No, ticklish."

Her lips form into a cute smile. "Oh, that's good to know," she says, her fingers tracing over my ribs, and I grab hold of her hand in mine.

"Careful, V, don't start something you won't be able to finish."

And I already know that's exactly what she's planning to do as she has this look in her eye. Before I even have time to stop her, she straddles me, her hands tickling my sides.

I squirm beneath her, and once I'm over the initial action, I sit up, taking her with me and grabbing her hands into one of mine, raising them above her head.

"Easy, V. If I do recall, you're the most ticklish of all," I say, blowing over the hollow of her throat. I love how her skin prickles with goosebumps, but mostly, I love seeing new ways her body reacts to my touch.

She fidgets in my hold, but there is no way I'm letting her off that easy, and with my free hand, I begin tickling her instead. She bucks at the contact, wriggling like crazy and giggling, the sound sending warmth through my entire body.

"I give up, stop," she says, breathless, once I have her beneath me again.

I let go of her hands and she moves them to my hips, and I wipe away the stray tear from her eyes.

"It's a good look on you, V, seeing you happy."

She smiles, her fingers tracing my scar again.

"And are you happy?"

I nod. "Yes, very." And it's the truth. Being with her brings me so much comfort it's unreal.

"Will you tell me about this?" she says, her fingers brushing over the raised skin of my scar.

I lay down beside her and she turns to face me, so we're both on our sides.

"You don't have to, only if you want to," she says gently.

If it were anyone else asking, I would probably evade the question, but not with Verity. I want her to know all the parts of me, even the bad and the ugly.

"It was from shrapnel, but I was lucky."

She wraps her fingers with my mine, urging me to continue.

"Others, not so much. I don't think I'll ever be able to unsee their faces, the way they looked at me to help our friend. And when I was staring down while chaos rained down all around, his eyes void of life, I already knew there was nothing I could do. It was instant."

I clear my throat. That was way too deep, even for me. It's still too raw, and I don't want to elaborate. I don't think I'll ever be able to articulate that day, not out loud. They say time is a healer, but not for him, and not for his family or his friends.

Taking a deep breath, I continue. "There was nothing I could do, it happened too quickly. One minute we were on patrol, the next all hell broke loose, and we were under fire."

Her eyes begin to glisten with unshed tears, and I pull her up until she's closer to me, and I stroke the back of her head.

"Oh my God, Liam. I'm sorry, I never knew, Callum never said you'd been hurt."

I shake my head. "He didn't know. I mean, he knew about me losing my friend, but he knows less than you do."

She worries her lip. "You can't keep it all bottled up though, Liam. You need to heal in here as well as here." One hand covers my heart, the other goes to my side.

"I'm working on it. Besides, you make everything better."

Her breath hitches and her eyes soften. "I don't know how but thank you for saying that."

I lean down until my lips are practically touching hers. "Just from being you. Your presence alone makes things better."

Pulling her closer, I love the hitch in her breathing as her centre meets my erection. The way her lips part and she licks over her full bottom lip is so fucking sensual.

Before I get lost in her, I force myself to get up and hold out my hand for her. "Come on."

"What? Where are we going?"

"First, we're going to shower, and then I want you to show me how this Cranked of yours works."

She takes my hand and I pull her up and onto her feet as she laughs. "It's a Cricut," she replies, smiling.

"Yeah, that's what I said."

"Of course you did." Her eyes scan the floor.

"What are you looking for?" I ask, following her line of sight.

"Something to put on," she says.

"Nuh uh." I shake my head. "We're just going across the hall to the bathroom, V, you don't need any clothes, believe me," I say, biting my lower lip as my eyes trail over her body.

"Says you." Her arm comes up and she attempts to cover her breasts, but I grab her wrists and hold out her arms either side of her body.

"Verity, I spent the last few hours getting even more acquainted with every single freckle, mole, and curve on your delectable body. You don't ever have to cover up, not for me."

She looks down between us, her cheeks heating as a flush breaks out over her throat.

"It's easy for you to say, you seem quite at home in your birthday suit."

"I'm just making the most of the time I have alone with you," I admit and let go of her and step back, slowly moving in a circle, and just when I know she has the perfect view of my backside, I clench my arse cheeks together.

The sound of a soft moan escapes her, and I peer over my shoulder. "You like what you see?"

Her tongue flicks out and wets her lips before she answers, causing my dick to twitch—what was semi hard is now a full-on boner.

"Yeah, I really do."

Without another word, I walk out into the hallway and into the bathroom. I love the sound of her bare feet as they softly pad across the carpet as she follows.

"You're right," she says, her naked body pressing against my back as she wraps her arm around my waist and takes hold of my hard length. "Let's make the most of the alone time while we can."

I let out a hiss between my teeth and let her show me exactly what she has in mind.

Chapter Thirty

Verity

I pause what I'm doing to look over at Liam. He has his tongue poking out of the corner of his mouth as he concentrates on weeding the vinyl design I gave him, and unable to help myself, I reach for my phone and snap a quick picture, causing the flash to go off.

"Shit."

His head shoots up, and he cocks an eyebrow.

"Sorry, not sorry," I say with a shrug.

Liam is up and by my side before I even take a breath, grabbing for my phone, and it takes a second for me to catch up as he holds the phone out above us.

"I prefer ones with you in them," he says. I try to duck out of the way, but he's too fast as he grabs my side and pulls me to his body. "Come on, not fair, you got a picture of me, it's only fair you take a selfie with me." He pouts and I find myself caving.

"Okay, fine." I look back to the phone.

"Cheese," he says, snapping a picture.

Looking at the picture, he airdrops it to himself and kisses my cheek before going back to the desk.

Unexpected Love

I open my camera roll and smile. It's actually a really nice picture—dare I say, I look happy.

"You know this weeding, it's quite therapeutic," he says as he continues his task. I have to give him credit, when I was showing him the machine, it all kind of went over his head. After watching me and asking questions for near on an hour, he asked if he could help, so I gave him the mandala design to weed, and he's been at it ever since.

"Well, there'll be plenty more of those, so I know who to come to when my hand is cramping."

"I still think you should come off Etsy and build a website."

I give a non-committal nod and mumble a "Maybe."

"It's fine if you're not quite ready to yet, but when you are, I'll help."

Glancing over to him, he's watching me. "You know about websites?" I ask.

He smiles and nods. "Yep. Who do you think helped Callum build his author website?"

I point to him. "You?"

"That I did. I'll have you know, I'm a dab hand when it comes to computers, websites, and social media. I looked at your Instagram page too, and I have to say, even I was impressed."

Tilting my head, I raise my eyebrows. "I don't know whether to be insulted or not."

His laugh sends butterflies straight to my lower belly.

"It was a compliment, believe me. I spent the best part of a year being an admin for Callum's. When I enlisted, he had to take over, and I'm proud to say Yoda taught him well."

I lean back in my chair. "Wow, you're quite full of yourself, and there was me thinking you didn't have any flaws."

His smile drops, and I instantly feel bad. "Oh, believe me, I have plenty of those."

Pushing to my feet, I go over and take his hand in mine. He leans back and pulls me into his lap.

"That might be true, but it's hard to see when it's your positive traits that call to me."

He bites his lower lip and his cheeks tinge with the slightest flush.

"Why, Liam Carmichael, are you blushing?"

I feel something akin to a growl and he stands up, me cradled in his arms, and goes over to the bed.

"You know, when you say my full name, it turns me the fuck on."

He drops me not so delicately on the mattress, and I kind of love it.

"As much as I love it when you go all cave man on me, Liam, I also know what you're doing." I pull his arm and lay back, patting the space beside me.

"You say you have plenty of flaws, but I think we might have very different ideas of what these are. Is it not you who keeps making me say positive affirmations about myself?"

He reaches out and wraps his hand over my thigh, his thumb moving in slow torturous circles, but I refuse to allow him to distract me from my chain of thought.

"Yes, I did."

My hand covers his and he stills his movement. "Well, I want you to start doing the same."

Scrunching his forehead, I can already see he's about to try and find a way to brush it off or just say he will, but he won't.

"I'm serious, Liam. You're good at helping others and offering them advice, but it works both ways, and you owe it to yourself to do the same for you."

His nostrils flare slightly when he lets out a heavy breath.

"Yeah, I know you're right. It's just so much goes on inside this head of mine."

"Can I ask you something? And please don't take this the wrong way when I do."

Smiling, he turns his hand over and links our fingers together.

"You are still getting help for your PTSD?"

I watch him lick his lips and swallow before he replies. "Yeah, I am. I was lucky to be fast tracked when I left the army. I have a therapist and they've moved my one-to-one therapy sessions via phone, and there are resources and an online support group I'm part of."

I let out a breath. "Okay, that's good, because the thought of you suffering in silence isn't something I can bear thinking about. You can always talk to me though, about anything, you know that, right?"

He nods and leans closer, until his lips are only a whisper away from mine. "I do, and likewise."

I make up the distance and kiss him. He rolls me onto my back and hovers over me as he slowly devours my mouth. This isn't like any other kiss we've shared before, there's so much more, it's full of something so much more profound than anything I've ever experienced before. It makes my heart race and my adrenaline spike. It's terrifying and exhilarating. And that's when it hits me… I am seriously falling head over heels for this man.

Chapter Thirty-One

Verity

I finally got news that my parents are allowed to come home, thank bloody goodness. They've been tested and are covid free, thankfully, but are showing symptoms. Luckily, they won't be quarantined, but do need to self-isolate when they come back home.

My dad has been holding back about their time on the ship while being kept to their cabin on their cruise—like always, they don't want us to worry.

"I'll go and pick them up," Liam says, coming up behind me and pulling me back against his chest.

"No, you don't have to do that, I'll go."

He rests his chin on my shoulder.

"No, let me, they have symptoms, and I don't want you to put yourself at risk."

I turn in his arms and link my hands behind his back.

"Oh, but it's okay that you do?"

He leans down and kisses the tip of my nose.

"I'm in-between jobs, you're not. Besides, I don't mind, they're family."

My heart squeezes in my chest. There isn't anything he wouldn't do, and yet, getting James to come to my parents' for

Sunday dinner was a fucking chore. I realise that Liam needs this, so I nod.

"Okay, I'll get you added to my car insurance."

My response garners a laugh from him, and I roll my eyes.

"What's funny?"

"Nothing at all, baby, I just love how your mind works."

My breath catches in my throat when his mouth captures mine in a powerful kiss, the kind song writers create lyrics about. My entire body floods with heat, every nerve ending coming to life.

When we both come up for air, I'm dizzy from the heat of the kiss.

"I'm not going to lie; I'll miss being able to do this whenever I want."

His lips move to my throat as he peppers me with tantalising sweet kisses.

"Same. Maybe we should make the most of today while we still can."

Liam hums his agreement, his lips causing the most delicious torture.

"You know, I've always fantasied about taking you right there on that table."

My lower stomach clenches and I squeeze my thighs together.

"Oh, maybe you should show me," I reply, feeling brazen and reckless in the moment.

"You want to be naughty with me, V?"

I think I nod because he grips the hem of my top. "Arms up then." And I comply immediately.

"I love it when you do what I say."

His lips cover the lace of my bra, sucking my nipple through the thin material, and I let out a groan.

Liam dips his hands into my jogging bottoms and cups me firmly.

"Fuck," I hiss out through my teeth.

No matter how he manhandles me, I am here for every fucking second of it. One thing I've come to know about Liam is he has an insatiable appetite when it comes to sex, something I am in no way complaining about—he matches my sexual drive perfectly.

He moves his lips to the shell of my ear and whispers, "Is your cunt wet for me?"

I swear my knees almost buckle. Love it when he talks to me like that.

"Want me to bend you over that table and see if we can bring my fantasy to life?"

Is that even a question? My nipples pebble underneath the lace of my bra as I let out a shiver.

"I'll take that as a yes."

He pulls his hand out of my joggers and brings his fingers to his nose as he draws back enough for me to see.

"You smell so fucking good all turned on for me, V."

It's as though I just received a dose of pure adrenaline as my heart rate increases and my chest rises and falls in quick succession as he drops to his knees and drags my bottoms down my legs. He picks up each foot for me to step out of them, and then he leans in and inhales.

"So fucking good."

His mouth clamps over my centre and I jerk into him, but he pulls away, rising to his feet and stepping back, picking up one of my hands in his.

"Turn," he says, circling his index finger in the air.

I slowly do as he asks, and he holds my hand above my head as I twirl slowly, and I hear him suck in a breath. Facing him again, I look down to see he's pulled his erection free from his boxers, the head glistening with pre-cum, and I lick my lips in anticipation of tasting him. He always tastes so fucking intoxicating.

Glancing up, I find his pupils dark as he pokes the inside

of his cheek with his tongue as his eyes continue to scan all over my body.

"Did you wear this underwear for me or for you?" he asks, his voice a deep baritone.

I want to say I wore it for him, but lately, I've been doing more things for me, and it feels fucking liberating.

"I wore it for me," I admit.

His smile is my undoing. "Good girl."

Pulling on my hand, he turns me so I'm facing the table.

He leans close, pulling my hair over my shoulder to expose my neck. "There is nothing more fucking sexy than seeing you own it. Your confidence turns me the fuck on, V."

His fingers trail down my arms until he gets to my hips and grips me, pulling me against his hard body, his hand coming around the front and slipping under the lace of my thong, his finger teasing my slit.

I lean back against him.

"You're wet for me. Do I turn you on as much as you do me?"

"Yes."

His finger moves, teasing my entrance, but then he pulls his hand away.

I tut my discontent.

"Take off your underwear. I want you bare to me."

Swallowing hard, my hands tremble as I lower my thong and step out of it and then reach behind my back to unclasp my bra. My breathing accelerates when I glance over my shoulder to find him already naked, his hard erection stiff in his hand.

"Face forward." His voice is a command. I turn away quickly and hold my breath as I listen to his quiet movements behind me.

I feel his foot tap my ankle. "Now spread your legs."

Doing as he asks, I close my eyes, about ready to self-combust as I wait for him to make his next move.

He doesn't keep me waiting as I feel the tip of his hard-on against on my lower back as his hands spread my arse cheeks, and then I feel his shaft settle between my legs, causing the most phenomenal friction.

"Oh my God."

And then his palm settles on the back of my neck, his hand gripping me firmly in place as he pushes me forward until my chest meets the solid oak tabletop, and my hips touch the edge of the table. I turn my face, resting my cheek against it and inhale the earthy and spicy aroma as my forearms and palms lay flat on either side of me.

Chapter Thirty-Two

Liam

Fucking hell, I'm about to explode. Having her like this has only ever been a fantasy, and having her like putty in my hands, so fucking compliant, it's even harder to keep my shit together and not cum just from the sight of her.

As much as I want to take her hard, she's pressed up against a solid oak table, and I don't want to hurt her. Marking her with my mouth and tongue is one thing, but I don't want to hurt her.

Taking myself in my hand again, I settle myself between her legs, teasing her wet entrance, her breathing coming out louder.

Leaning over her, I whisper in her ear, "Stay still and don't move."

Slowly, inch by excruciating inch, I enter her. Her hot channel clenches my shaft as I do—it's the best kind of fucking torture, and I keep going until I bottom out.

"Fuck," I hiss out through my teeth. "I love how your cunt takes my cock."

Her channel clenches around me again, and she's panting now.

I roll my hips slowly, loving how she doesn't move, even

though her fingers flex over the smooth surface beneath her nails, tapping against the hardwood as she does.

Pulling almost all the way out, I thrust back into her as slow as my resolve will allow. I repeat the same move until I feel her entire body tensing, coiling tight, as she goes on her tip toes, unable to keep still any longer.

"You're desperate to move, aren't you?" She moves her head just a fraction. I pull out, even though it pains me to do so. "I want to see your face, turn around."

Verity pushes up onto her hands as I walk over to the sofa and grab a cushion. When I return, she's facing me, her chest rising and falling.

Without prompting, she sits on the edge of the table and moves back. "Lift," I say, holding out the cushion in my hand. She looks to it and then to me. "We can wash it if we need to."

She lifts her pelvis and I slide it beneath her and step between her legs as she rests back on her elbows.

Taking hold of her hips, I position her right where I want her, before taking myself in my hand, settling at her entrance, holding her hips tightly as I push inside with a hard thrust.

Her hands grip the edge of the table, her eyes locked on mine. I look between us and watch the way my dick slides inside her—her cunt fits my cock to the point of perfection. She moves her hands to hold on to my forearms, her entire body moving, rocking back and forth.

"Wrap your legs around my body," I grunt out between thrusts. "And lock your ankles."

I lean forward, the penetration so deep I pause and take a deep breath as she clenches around me. "Arms around my neck."

Moving into a standing position, I support her body and make my way over to the alcove just under the stairs and press her gently back against the wall.

"Do you know how badly I wanted to fuck you against this wall that night?"

We're both covered in a sheen of sweat.

"No, but I'm starting to get the idea," she says, breathless, licking her lips.

Needing to sit, I hold her securely in my arms and step away from the wall and make my way over to the armchair and sit down with her still wrapped around me. Her eyes never once leave mine.

She begins to rock into me, and the feeling is so much more intense. I try to slow my breathing, the build-up of sensations growing so much more intense the longer I hold her to me. The way she looks into my eyes… it's on a deeper level. And I know I will die loving this woman, from this life to the next, there isn't a doubt in my mind.

She continues rocking into me and I let her take the control. Pulling her down so I can whisper those three words I've always wanted to say.

"I love you, Verity Warren." It's barely about a whisper but the way her breath hitches lets me know she's heard, and then I lower my lips and my mouth clamps down on her neck and I suck, needing to mark her. She tilts her head, giving me even more access.

When I draw back, I hold her gaze until I know we're both past the point of no return.

"Oh." Her mouth forms the perfect 'O' as her walls flutter around my cock, her orgasm taking hold, and she rocks into me, milking my cock as she comes, throwing her head back. I don't want this to end, but my release is fast, and I come deep inside her as her inner walls continue to spasm all over me.

My head falls back against the chair, and I keep her where she is until the aftershocks of her orgasm begin to ease off.

She rests her forehead on my shoulder, and I reach up, gripping her jaw until she's looking at me.

"I meant what I said, V."

She nods, her eyes glistening. "I know."

And then she kisses me slow and sweet.

When she pulls out of the kiss, she begins to giggle.

"I can't believe we did that. I don't think I'll ever be able to sit at the table or walk in here and not think of you and me."

I wink. "That's the idea. And just so you know, if I had my way, I'd fuck you on every surface in every room of this house."

She scrunches up her nose. "I can get behind most rooms, except any of my brothers' or my parents'," she says with a shudder. "That's just icky."

"Come on, we should go clean up. Unless you like to be full of my cum," I whisper against her ear.

The response is her clenching around my semi hard dick, and I raise an eyebrow.

"Or we could sit here and go again in another five minutes."

"As much as I could get behind that, the thought of my parents coming back and the house smelling like a sex parlour isn't on my to-do list."

I reach out and caress her breasts. "Too late."

She arches her back, and I love how sensitive her nipples are. She loves it when I play with them.

"In that case, make me come again, Liam."

Verity doesn't have to ask me twice. She shifts as I sit forward and places her palms on my thighs as I reach between us and play with her clit, her channel tightening around me, causing me to grow hard all over again. She rolls her hips, and together we get lost in oblivion.

Chapter Thirty-Three

Verity

I can't keep still as I wait for my parents to get home with Liam. As soon as I hear the car pull up on the drive, I'm at the front door.

My dad gets out first, and like he always does, he goes around to open my mum's door, holding out his hand to help her out.

Liam is already opening the boot and retrieving the suitcases. I presume he says he'll get them as they both walk up the path. I can't see their mouths because they're wearing masks, but I'm sure they're smiling and just happy to be home. Instinctively, I go to step out and hug them, and then have to stop myself. They'll both be self-isolating until they are symptom free.

"Verity," my dad says. "Good to see you, princess."

"You too, Dad. I'm glad you're both home. Hi, Mum."

I step out of the way so they can enter.

"Hi, sweetie. Please tell me you have the kettle on, I'm parched."

Smiling, I nod. "Of course. Go on up and I'll bring them up for you."

Luckily, they have the top floor bedroom suite, with a

bathroom. Anything has to be better than that tiny cabin they were confined to.

"It's so good to be home," my mum gushes as they both make their way upstairs.

I go outside and take one of the suitcases from Liam as he removes his mask. I go up on tiptoes and kiss his cheek. He looks surprised by the action, but in a good way.

"Thank you."

He shakes his head. "You don't have to thank me. I'm just glad they're both home and safe. From the sound of it, no one knew their earhole from their arsehole."

He lifts both suitcases over the front doorstep and I take them through to the utility room. I'll wash everything after I've made everyone some lunch.

We both go over to the sink at the same time, and I smile when he ushers me to wash my hands first before he washes his.

"Do you want a cup of tea?"

"Please." I see him shake his hands in my peripheral vision and pass him the tea towel.

I line up the mugs and tap the counter as I wait for the kettle to boil.

Liam pulls me against his chest and leans his chin on my shoulder. And we stand there in comfortable silence.

"You know, I never had this with James." He automatically tenses, so I turn in his arms.

"I never realised how jealous you were until now."

A low rumble leaves his chest. "Not jealous, you're not with him. What have I got to be jealous about?"

I link my hands behind his back, holding him tightly.

"Absolutely nothing. And all I meant is, I find inner peace when I'm with you. I never had that with him."

He smiles and relaxes; his face softens as he lowers his face and kisses my nose as the kettle clicks.

"Well, I'll take that as a compliment."

I let go of him and turn away to make the tea when the milk appears beside me.

"Thank you."

"No worries. What's in the oven?" he asks.

"Lasagne. I figured they'd be hungry, so made Dad's favourite."

I drain the tea bags from each mug before adding a dash of milk and then sugar to my mum's and mine.

"You know, you're sweet enough already."

Laughing, I grab one of the beanbag trays and add my parents' tea, along with a packet of Mum's favourite Bourbon biscuits.

"Really? You like sweet, do you?"

He lowers his head until his lips graze my cheek, right before he answers, "Only outside of the bedroom." Kissing my cheek, he steps back and winks. I have no doubt I'm blushing as my face heats from his words.

Keeping my hands steady, I pick up the tray.

"Here, let me carry it," he says, and before I can object, he's taken it out of my hold and is already heading towards the stairs. I follow, and then in the hallway, I go around him as he places it outside the door as I rap on it with the back of my knuckles.

"Room service."

I step back so we are a few feet away, and my dad pops his head out, mask and all, as he retrieves the tray.

"Thanks, princess."

"You welcome, Barry," replies Liam.

I swat him and he grabs me around the waist as his fingers move to tickle me.

"Don't you dare," I say around a giggle as I wriggle in his hold.

My dad clears his throat and Liam instantly lets go, running his hand through his hair.

"I'll go get your holiday washing started," I say, my skin on fire as I turn away and head back downstairs.

I don't notice Liam catch up to me until he touches my shoulder and I let out a ridiculous sounding squeal and then burst out laughing.

"Sorry, I didn't mean to embarrass you in front of your dad," he says, rubbing the back of his neck. My nervous laughter dies on my lips when I see his expression. I move into his space and place my hands on his hips.

"You didn't. It's just when you touch me, it's hard to focus on anything else."

My words earn me a smile, and he lowers his lips to mine. The kiss quickly becomes heated, but he's the one to pull away first, resting his forehead against mine as we both catch our breath.

"This is going to be torture. Even more so now I know what it's like to have you all to myself."

I can't disagree with him there. "Well, just think, as soon as lockdown is eased, my house should be ready, so there's always that to look forward to."

We head back into the kitchen and grab our tea just as the oven starts beeping.

"Now that's what I call perfect timing," he says, rubbing his stomach.

He doesn't miss a beat though as he gets out a stack of plates from the cupboard and then starts rummaging in the cutlery drawer. He's so at ease here, and I wonder if that will change once my parents and brothers find out we're... together.

Shit, I'm with Liam Carmichael.

Chapter Thirty-Four

Liam

It's been a busy week and a half with Verity's parents, Linda and Barry, both self-isolating, but today is their first day of freedom—well, as much as lockdown will allow, that is that they finally get the whole house back and the use of the garden too.

This also means as of tonight, if I want to sleep in V's room, I'll be sneaking out in the morning. She hasn't said about telling them yet and I don't want to pressure her, I can go as slow or as fast as she wants, just as long as I get to be with her, that's all I care about.

"So, you're all being Furloughed?" Barry asks Verity.

"Yeah, for now at least."

"Well, at least you'll still get paid," her dad replies.

I squeeze her knee under the table and watch as her cheeks bloom a soft shade of red.

"Yeah, there's that."

She brings her spoonful of yogurt and granola to her mouth and pauses, looking at me from the corner of her eye, her lip curving into a small smile.

"I think you should get a website up and running and start

putting your stuff out there," I say as I stuff a piece of croissant into my mouth.

"What's that for?" Linda asks, putting down her mug.

Verity is positively on fire now; she looks down at her bowl, and I hate how she withdraws like that.

"It's just something I started doing when I broke up with James," she says, her voice low. "It's nothing special."

I shake my head and place my arm over the back of her chair.

"I call bullshit," I say and earn a laugh from her mum.

"And that's why you're my favourite son," Linda says.

Verity raises her head with a mock eye roll. "Don't let Callum hear you say that. The baby would have a fit."

I notice her shoulders tense, her face turning to me, and then back to her mum. I've always felt like part of the family, and they've always treated me like a son. I remove my arm from the back of Verity's chair and shift in my seat and reach over to collect the empty plates and push my chair back so I can give myself a minute.

I sense Verity before she even speaks, and turn to face her. "Shit, I'm sorry," she says, placing her now empty bowl in the dishwasher.

"Why are you sorry?" I say, crossing my arms.

"Calling Callum a baby," she says, worrying her bottom lip.

"You don't have to apologise for that. I was just wondering if your mum would have the same opinion of me if she knew about us." I point between the two of us.

"She'll be made up, Liam, you're the child she never had."

I laugh. "Well, that's saying a lot, seeing as there's five of you," I reply.

"Exactly, and not one of us is you."

She surprises me when she steps into my body and wraps her arms around my back.

"Stop it, you'll make me blush," I say, resting my chin on

the crown of her head. God, she always smells so sinfully exquisite.

"Good payback for you throwing me under the bus back in there."

I grip the top of her arms and push her back gently so I can see her face.

"Hardly throwing you under the bus. You're allowed to pursue your passion, Verity. And if you ask me, now is the perfect time. When else would you have this kind of free time to build a website and upload your merchandise?"

She rests her palms on my chest. "You make it sound so easy."

I shake my head and grip her jaw. "I never said anything about it being easy. I'm just saying, why not use this opportunity to do something for you? I believe in you, V. I wish you believed in yourself too."

She inhales a deep breath and straightens. "Do you know what? You're right. What else is there to do?"

"Me," I reply with a wink. Smacking my chest, she steps away just as Barry enters.

And she makes herself busy tidying up the counter.

"Have you decided what you'll do now you're a civilian again?" Barry asks as Verity takes the dishes and empty mugs from him.

I nod. "Yeah, I've been looking at getting a degree in physiotherapy. I still want to be able to help people," I reply with a shrug, and stuff my hands into my pockets.

"Have you applied?" Verity asks, pausing what she's doing.

"I have. Hopefully, all being well, I'll start in September."

She smiles and stops what she's doing to come over to me and gives me a quick hug. "That's amazing, Liam. I didn't know that was something you wanted to do."

I clear my throat. "Yeah, I've been looking online and talking to my advisor at CTP."

When she pulls away, it takes me a second to try and not

let myself drag her back to my body—the only reason I let her go is because her dad is standing right there.

He reaches out his hand and shakes mine. "That's wonderful, son. You'll make a great physiotherapist."

"Thank you, Barry."

After he's left the room, Verity comes back and stands in front of me.

"Why didn't you tell me?" she asks, her expression hurt a little, and I instantly feel bad.

I pull her between my legs and wrap my arms around her waist. "I was still trying to decide if it was what I wanted to do. I wasn't keeping it from you, honest, I hadn't even mentioned it to Callum."

She relaxes in my hold. "That's fair enough, but you know you can talk to me about anything, right? It's a two-way street, you and me."

I nod. "I know, thank you." Lowering my mouth to hers, I give her a chaste kiss on the lips, and as usual, she tastes delicious.

"And just so you know, I think you'll do amazing."

"Thank you. All I need to do now is sort my living arrangements out."

Verity pulls back, tilting her head. "You know my parents will let you stay here as long as you need, there's no rush."

I nod. "Yeah, but honestly, I want to be able to get you alone and have you screaming my name in pure ecstasy."

Her cheeks flush and she bites down on her lower lip.

"Oh, is that so?" she says playfully.

"Very much so."

"Well, in that case, best you hurry up."

Laughing, I lunge for her and she lets out a small squeal as I lift her off her feet.

"Anyone would think you're trying to get rid of me," I joke.

She shakes her head and I'm hit with the sweet scent of her perfume.

"Hardly. I just like the idea of you making me scream."

I pull her hard against my erection.

"Fuck, Verity, you're killing me."

Her sensual giggle is like an added aphrodisiac, and I have to let her go, otherwise there is no way in hell I'm leaving this kitchen without sporting a king-size boner.

Chapter Thirty-Five

Verity

I feel like a naughty kid with Liam sneaking out of my room every morning, but it's also kind of exciting. Other than James, I never had anyone else in my childhood room.

Walking him to my door, he gives me a quick peck on the lips before slipping out. Just as I'm about to close it after him, he stops it with his foot and leans back in and gives me a morning kiss to remember.

When he pulls back, he gives me a devilish smile and I watch him as he walks towards Callum's room, appreciating his arse right before he slips inside.

"You know he doesn't have to keep sneaking out of your room."

I jump and let out a squeal of surprise and turn to find my dad carrying a cup of tea, no doubt for my mum. My hand goes to my chest, my heart beating a mile a minute. "Shit, Dad. You scared the crap out of me," I say over a nervous laugh.

He smirks back in response. "Well, your mum and I want you to know the two of you don't have to sneak around or hide whatever it is between you."

I raise an eyebrow. "And if we were just, you know…

you'd be okay with that?" My cheeks heat because as close as I am to my dad, no daughter wants to talk about their sex life with their father.

"As long as you're happy and safe, you get no judgement from me or your mother."

I sniff, my nose tingling. Damn it, it's way too early to get all emotional.

"Thank you, but just so you know, it's more than just that... we're together."

He smiles. "Yeah, we know."

Shaking my head, I laugh. "Why didn't you say anything?"

"Because we figured you both would when you were ready. Besides, I've always seen how he looks at you, but now I see you looking at him in the same way. It didn't exactly take a genius to work it out."

I worry my bottom lip. "So, you're both cool with it?" I ask, staring down at my bed socks.

He nods and comes over, wrapping his free arm over my shoulder and kissing the crown of my head.

"Of course, why wouldn't we be?"

"I guess because he's Callum's best friend, and the age gap."

My dad squeezes my shoulder gently. "Do either of those things bother you?"

I shake my head. "No, not at all. I just hope Callum is okay with it."

"And if he isn't?"

I clear my throat. "Then that's on him and not on us."

When I tilt my head to look at my dad, he's smiling. He looks so much like Callum, just an older version.

"Then that's all that matters." He lets go and steps away. "I best get your mum her tea before she starts to get the arse ache with me."

He starts walking down the hallway and then looks back over his shoulder.

"And, princess…"

I pause in my doorway.

"It's good to see you more like yourself again."

This time, my eyes fill with tears, but I blink them away. "Thank you, Dad. It feels good," I admit.

He gives me a knowing nod and continues up the stairs to their room.

I retrieve my phone from my bedside table and send Liam a text.

Me: Looks like the cats out of the bag…

I smile when bubbles appear pretty much instantly.

Liam: What cat would that be?

Me: My mum and dad know about us. They said we don't have to hide it and you can stop sneaking out of my room.

Waiting for his reply, nothing comes, and then my bedroom door is opening.

"Well, in that case…"

I laugh as he throws himself on the bed beside me, almost falling off in the process. I can't wait to be in my own place and get back to a king-size bed again.

"Did you tell them?" he asks, mirroring me and laying on his side, his hand going to my thigh as he pulls it over his leg.

"No, Dad saw you leaving my room just now. He said we didn't need to hide."

His eyes sparkle. "Oh, man, bet that was awkward."

I shake my head. "He nearly gave me a heart attack. But no, he was good about it, to be fair. Said he always saw how you looked at me and they saw how I've been looking at you." My cheeks heat.

"And how might that be?" he asks, leaning forward to kiss my nose before pulling back.

"Apparently how you look at me," I counter back.

"Which is?"

"Probably like I'm falling for you," I admit.

Unexpected Love

He gives me a toothy grin in response. "Well, it's not the same then, because I already fell."

I don't have a chance to reply because my phone vibrates between us, causing me to jump.

"Fuck," I say around a laugh.

He pulls it from the mattress between us and hands it to me, not even curious as to who would be messaging me at seven o'clock in the morning.

Maxine: I have a friend who I recommended you to and they want to know if you do custom orders? And I mean a *huge* order.

"Oh my God." I sit up so fast and almost shove Liam off in the process. "Shit, sorry."

"What is it?" he asks as I type back, and knowing he won't look without my say so, I angle the phone towards him as I type back.

Me: Yeah, of course I can, wow. And thank you xox

Maxine: No thanks needed, you're wasted at that boring arse firm and you know it.

Me: What, and you're not?

Liam pulls me to his side and kisses my temple.

"That's amazing, V. See? You're already in demand."

I can feel myself blushing as heat works over my face.

Maxine: Well, that's different… besides we're not all as multi-talented as you, love.

Me: You are very talented.

Maxine: Why? What's Nick told you?

Confused, I glance to Liam, who looks as confused as I do.

Me: Nothing, furloughed, remember? Why? What's going on with you and Nick?

Maxine: Never mind, I already gave them your email, so keep your eyes open.

Me: Okay, cool. Thank you, but just an FYI, you and I need to have a chat about you and Nick.

I come out of WhatsApp and go to my email, and sure enough, there's a query about custom options.

"Shit." I tilt my phone so Liam can read it too, and before I have a chance to even digest it, he's on his feet and holding out his hand for me.

"What?"

"We need to get you fed. You have a busy few days on the horizon and times a ticking."

I laugh and let him pull me up and into his arms.

"I haven't even replied to them yet."

"I'll make breakfast while you reply. Then I will be your weeding bitch or anything else you need." He bows. "I am at your service."

As excited as I already am, his enthusiasm is intoxicating and gives me an extra burst of energy. I jump up and down on the spot and do a happy dance.

Chapter Thirty-Six

Liam

It's been nearly two months of being in lockdown, and finally, restrictions are being eased, which is good, because I can't wait to get Verity alone and all to myself. It's tricky being under the same roof as her parents and restraining from taking her when I want and how I want has been hard.

She's no longer on furlough and is back to working from home, so between that and her small business taking off like crazy, it's been all hands-on deck. I enrolled and was accepted into King's College London, which I start in September, all being well, of course.

But I'm desperate to have some quality time with Verity as a couple, so I've planned to take her on our first official date on Saturday—not that she knows, I want it to be a surprise. I enter Verity's room and don't see her but hear her moving behind the partition of her walk-in wardrobe. It's so small you can barely have two people standing side by side. Apart from the drawers, it's all open, with a rail for all her clothes on hangers, and everything has its place from shoes to bags.

Best nook ever created. If we ever had a house of our own, I'd have her an entire room as a walk-in wardrobe.

And there I go again, getting ahead of myself.

"There you are."

I walk up to her and wrap my arms around her half naked body and pull her back against my chest.

"I think you should just wear this," I say, moving her hair off her shoulder and kissing her neck.

"I'm not sure that would be appropriate in front of my parents," she says, her voice a breathy whisper as I continue to pepper kisses over her throat and across her neck.

"I won't lie, this whole ordeal has given me a new appreciation for restraint when it comes to you."

Glancing up, I stare at our reflection in the mirror and notice her nipples are hard beneath the lace of her bra.

I love the way she pushes back against me, her breathing becoming louder in the confines of the small space.

"I need to look at places to rent so I can take you any way I want, and whenever I want."

"Is that so?" she says, her eyelids fluttering closed as a flush works over her exposed skin.

I lean closer and whisper in her ear, "Absolutely. There isn't a surface that won't be left untouched by me fucking you into a state of oblivion."

Her lips form a smile.

"Wow, you're cocksure of yourself."

I press my erection up against her arse and she gasps, her eyes springing open.

"It's a fact, V."

Her expression changes as she stares back at our reflection, my fingers trailing a path over her stomach and to the waistband of her lacy thong.

"Then how about you prove it?" she says in challenge.

I spin her until her back is flush against the wall and press my body to hers.

"Oh, believe me, I want to." I lower my face, nip at her jaw, and then I pepper kisses down her throat.

"Do it."

Unexpected Love

Pulling back, I look into her eyes to see her pupils are dilated.

"Your parents are downstairs, so if we do this, you need to be quiet."

Having lazy morning sex with her and keeping quiet is one thing, but this, taking her right here will be something else entirely.

"What if you're the one who can't keep quiet?" she says.

I cock an eyebrow, because I won't lie, when I'm deep inside her, it's easy to lose all my inhibitions.

"Or are you politely trying to tell me you don't want me?" She fake pouts and puts her hand on my chest, ready to push me away, but I grip them in one hand like a shackle and raise her arms above her head.

"I always want you." I thrust into her, and she lets out a small moan.

Using my free hand, I slip it under the material of her thong and stroke my finger between her wet folds.

"Hmm, so ready for me," I say and kiss her throat as I tease her entrance and then hook my finger inside her. I start fucking her with my finger, and as her breathing picks up, I add another, giving her more of what she needs. And then when I feel her writhing against the palm of my hand, trying to get more friction, I pull my fingers free, and her eyes spring open.

"Easy, baby, I'll make you come. I just need you to bend over," I say. Letting go of her hands, I turn her so she's facing the wardrobe and so my back is now pressed against the wall. I see her shiver at the sound of my zipper as I undo my jeans, and freeing myself from my boxers, I kick them off at my ankles.

"It's going to be a tight fit, baby, you ready?"

She nods and looks over her shoulder, her eyes roaming down to my erection that I'm squeezing in my hand.

"Thong off and bend over."

Shimming out of her underwear, she faces forward and bends over, her arse in the air, as she rests her hands level with her face on the bottom of the shelf.

Kicking her legs further apart, I position myself at her entrance and glance over to the full-length mirror to my left and grip her hip, watching myself as I thrust into her. Her hands slide against the surface of the wood and she has to push herself back against me to keep from being lost in the clothing.

"Oh God," she groans.

"You know, I have the perfect side view of your cunt taking my cock."

She turns her head so she can see the mirror.

"Oh shit," she says, licking her lips. Her eyes focus on our joined bodies as I continue to give short, hard thrusts.

I reach around and start circling her clit. Her channel tightens and flutters around my engorged head.

As much as I love watching this, I need more, so I pull out and she lets out a whimper.

"Belly down on the floor," I say, pointing to the fluffy rug.

She swallows, looks at me and then the floor and gets down on her knees before laying on her stomach, her face to the side and arms either side of her head.

I lie down on top of her, keeping my weight off, and then slide back into her from behind.

"Shit," she mumbles.

"You okay?" I ask, because I know how this position gives super deep penetration, but I don't want it to hurt.

"Yeah, just so full."

She reaches back and wraps her hand around my shaft to help control how deep I go, and I suck my bottom lip between my teeth, letting out a deep groan. But when she changes the angle of her arse, I pretty much lose my shit.

"Oh fuck, Verity."

I bow my head forward as the sensations hit every nerve

ending in my body and reach around to start circling her clit, desperate for us both to find our release together.

Her breaths are coming out in deep puffs of air as we both climb higher and higher.

"Fuck, fuck, fuck," she hisses through her teeth.

And just like that, my balls squeeze tight, and then we both shatter. Her pulsing channel strangles my dick as I erupt inside her, in long hot spurts, filling her as she continues to spasm around my cock and I continue with short, fast thrusts.

When I'm spent, I pull out, my cum dripping out of her pussy, and unable to help myself, I lower my face and lick up the length of her, tasting our mixed pleasure. I pull back and fall onto my side, my back hitting the wall as she rolls onto her back, her chest rising and falling.

"Holy shit," she says, turning her face towards me, her face flushed. "That was…"

"Fucking hot," I finish for her, and she starts to giggle.

Chapter Thirty-Seven

Verity

I push myself up onto my elbows and look around for something to clean myself up enough to make a beeline for the bathroom.

"Here." In an expert move that makes my lower belly flutter all over again, Liam uses one hand and pulls his T-shirt off over his head and passes it to me.

He uses his boxers to wipe over his cock as I quickly clean between my legs and then move to stand up. I wobble on my feet and have to put my hand out to steady myself.

"Woah."

Liam is next to me, his hand on my waist. "Fuck, V, are you okay?"

I smile and reach out to stroke his cheek. "I'm fine, just haven't eaten yet, and I think you just zapped the last of my energy."

He frowns and grabs my dressing gown, passing it to me, before pulling on his jeans and leaving the top button undone, giving me the perfect view of his Adonis belt.

"Stop that, you need to eat."

I wiggle my eyebrows and he shakes his head. "Not me. Food." Leaning down, he kisses my forehead.

"Come on, let's get you in the shower, quick."

Tilting my head back, I look at his expression. "Oh, so now you don't want to shower with me?"

"I always want to shower with you. But I also don't want to disrespect your parent's hospitality by doing you in the shower."

I bite my lower lip and arch an eyebrow. "Oh, but fucking me against the shaggy rug was okay?"

His cheeks begin to heat, and I feel bad for winding him up.

"I'm playing. I love how you give a shit about my parents. God knows James never did."

His eyes spring to mine and his jaw clenches.

"Sorry," I say, looking away.

He grabs my chin and angles my face until I'm staring back at him.

"Why are you sorry?"

I swallow and lick my lips and fidget on the spot.

"I know you don't like it when I mention him."

Liam shakes his head. "No, he's your past and I know he got inside here." He brings his index finger to my temple and taps it gently. "And I hate that I wasn't able to protect you, but as long as I'm in here"—he lays his palm over my heart—"then that's all that matters."

I cover his hand with mine, but I don't even know how to respond to that, because he is, of course he is, but I'd be lying if I said I wasn't terrified of how he makes me feel.

"Surely you get it by now, Verity? I loved you before I even knew what it was to be in love. I sat back and watched you, hoping one day you'd look up and finally notice me." He pulls me to his body. "I don't care about the age gap. I don't care that Callum is my best friend and like a brother to me." He reaches out and caresses my cheek, his hand trembling. My ears thump loudly with the beating of my erratic heart. He bends his knees, so we're eye level. "But to make it clear, you've never been like a sister to me, Verity. You're the love of my life, so yes, I've slept with other women, had some light relationships, but I was never going to settle down and grow roots with them because I always had hope you'd find your way to me eventually."

His fingers graze down to my necklace and then to my locket, the pad of his thumb stroking over the word 'cariad'.

When I look back up, he's focused on me. "But your happiness will always come above mine. So, if you decide this is too much too soon and you don't want me the way I want you, it will fucking gut me, but I would never coerce you to be with me, not ever."

I swallow down the lump in my throat.

"It's not that. Of course I want to, but if we're being honest, I don't know what you see in me, Liam. And I worry that one day you'll wake up and realise I'm no more special than the next person."

He shakes his head, but I hold my hand up to stop him.

"Please, I need to get this out."

He gives a small nod and I continue—always so patient with me.

"I think there's this preconceived notion that things are easy for me, even more so when my weight is down," I say, using air quotes. "That I don't have insecurities or self-confidence issues, because I do."

It's probably why I knew the friends I thought were friends weren't. The amount of times I would hear, 'It's all right for you, you haven't had children. You're not married. You're slim. You have perfect skin.' The list is endless.

I sit down on the edge of the sofa, my body weary. "Do you know that I hate looking at myself in the mirror? Despise having my photo taken. But when I'm with you it's bearable, and I'm starting to love myself again. James used my insecurities against me all the time—whether we were alone or together, it didn't matter."

His hands cup my face as his thumbs wipe underneath my eyes at tears I can no longer control. I didn't realise how all my issues from being with James were eating me up inside. I can't even look at him now.

"Do you know I'd rarely be without makeup around him? I'd take it off right before going to bed. How pathetic is that?"

I can feel the tension radiating from Liam, and I feel bad we just had phenomenal sex and I'm having some sort of emotional breakdown.

"He's pathetic, he never fucking deserved you, V."

He's right, I know that now.

"It's crazy. I'd put up with it for so long and then one night we were watching TV and he spent the entire hour of the show commenting on the appearance of every person. All he saw were flaws, and all I could see was their beauty, their uniqueness. And I had an epiphany. This man could potentially be the father to my children, and could I really sit idly by and watch him crucify them?"

Liam's face takes on a hard edge, and even I feel nervous.

"I never knew half that shit, V. If I had, I don't think I could have sat back. I thought you were happy with him, and your happiness is my priority. So, if you need time to find yourself again, I can take a step back. I don't want you to feel like you're suffocated."

I smile. Even now, he's only thinking of me.

"I have found myself, though." I take his hand in mine, his calloused palm such a comforting touch against mine. "Don't you see? You gave me the strength I needed to believe in *me* again. And you don't suffocate me, not in the way you might think. Sometimes, when I'm with you, it's hard to breathe, but I wonder if it's because until you, I was doing it wrong." I shake my head. Trying to give words to the voices in my head is hard to articulate, and I love how even now, when I'm struggling to express as much, he is so damn patient.

"My heart beats differently with you than it ever has before, and it's not just a fleeting skip of my heart, either."

Bringing his hand to my chest, I hold his palm there. "Do you feel that? How hard my heart beats around you, like it's trying to break free from my chest, but only because it desperately wants to be whole, with you."

His smile wrecks me, but in the best possible way. Three words are on the edge of my tongue, but I don't have a moment to voice them when his lips crash down on mine, taking me in an all-consuming kiss.

Chapter Thirty-Eight

Verity

"You're home." My mum rushes over to Callum as soon as he steps through the threshold.

"Did you do a lateral flow test?" she asks as he closes the front door behind him.

He nods. "Of course, all good. Sorry it's late," he replies, looking over at the clock—it's almost ten thirty. He opens his arms for her to step in, and he gives her a hug.

"Don't be daft, we didn't know you were coming back is all, you should have told us you were on your way, anything could have happened."

He cringes at that. "Sorry, I wasn't thinking."

My dad pushes himself up from his armchair and gives him a hug and a pat on the back too.

"Good to have you home, son."

When my dad moves out of the way, it's my turn for a hug.

"Hey, V." He steps back and looks around.

"Where's Liam?"

Just then, he walks out of the kitchen with my mum and dad's tea and places them on the small coffee table. Every night since they've been back from their cruise, he makes them a cup of tea, along with a plate of their favourite biscuits. He's such a kiss arse, but in the best possible way. James never did anything remotely nice for them, not ever.

"Hey, man." Callum goes over and gives him a quick hug, and my cheeks heat suddenly from feeling nervous. We haven't told him yet about us, and out of nowhere, my anxiety is on high alert.

"Everything all right?" Liam asks as he steps back and takes in my brother's appearance.

He does look more dishevelled than usual, and he looks like he could do with some sleep.

"Not really," Callum replies as he drops down into what was my spot on the sofa.

"Uh oh, trouble in paradise?" Dad asks, half joking.

"Yep." Scrubbing his palm over his face, he lets out a groan and then pushes himself to his feet. "Anyway, I feel gross, I'm going to go grab a shower." He goes back towards the door for his suitcase and bag, lugging them upstairs with him.

"Wonder what all that's about?" Mum says, looking at my dad as she dunks a biscuit into her tea.

"I'm going to go see if he's all right," I say and follow him.

Even if I didn't hear Liam behind me, I'd feel his presence, and getting to the top of the landing, I wait for him. He gives me a quick kiss on the temple before we go to Callum's room.

The doors open, so we both just walk in as he rifles through his suitcase for his toiletry bag.

"I take it things didn't go well with Quinn?" Liam says as he leans against Callum's desk.

He looks up from what he's doing and shakes his head.

"Nope, and now I need to find a way to fix it, and stat." Callum moves to his feet and goes over to his bed and sits on the edge, his elbows on his knees.

"Maybe she just needs a day or two?" I suggest. Liam pulls

out the desk chair and spins it around for me to sit, and I smile, feeling my cheeks warm from the gesture.

"Thank you."

He winks, and I look away.

"Sorry, man, I didn't even think to text that I was coming home tonight, I can just take the couch or the floor," Callum says to Liam.

I watch as Liam rubs the back of his neck, it's a nervous tick of his, and I find myself holding my breath as he shakes his head.

"No, you're cool, I... ermm... haven't been sleeping in here," he says, his eyes moving from Callum to me, and I give the slightest of nods to let him know it's okay to tell him.

"Oh. What, have you found somewhere then?" Callum asks, frowning.

Liam swallows. Shit, he looks so nervous. I'm tempted to step in, but I think Liam needs to be the one to do this, they're best friends after all.

He shakes his head. "No, not exactly, I've been in V's room."

There's a pause before he replies, and Callum looks at me. "Oh, are you in your new house? You didn't say anything."

Now it's my turn to be nervous. "No, not for another couple of weeks."

He frowns, a 'V' forming between his brows as he sits up a little straighter.

"Back up... so what are you both trying to tell me here?" Callum's eyes flick between us.

"We're together—V and me," Liam blurts out in a rushed breath.

Callum moves to his feet. Shit. Has he always been that tall? Why do I suddenly feel really intimidated?

Liam follows suit, and now they're what... having a stand-off or something?

"As in, you're sleeping with my sister?"

I look to Liam for his reaction, and he raises his eyebrows. "Yes. Like I said, we're together."

"Since when?"

I fidget in the chair, the leather creaking beneath me, sweat forming between my shoulders.

"Since lockdown."

Callum turns away, walks towards his door, and then spins around again.

"So, you've been together all this time? You and my sister?"

I nod and bite the inside of my cheek, my heart racing as Liam replies, "Yeah."

He shakes his head and looks down at the floor before raising his eyes again.

"Boyfriend, girlfriend together? You're not just... you know?"

Is he seriously asking that?

"No, we're not just..." Liam clears his throat. "I'm serious about her."

Callum nods right before he breaks out into the biggest smile.

"About fucking time."

I exhale, my heart going pitter patter.

"So, you're cool with it?" Liam asks, and I can already hear the relief in his voice.

He pulls Liam in for a quick hug. "Of course. If anyone deserves her, it's you."

My chest squeezes. "Get in here," Callum says. I move to my feet, and he pulls me into the hug.

When he steps back, he points to us both. "You better be good to each other. Because I don't want to have to choose if the shit hits the fan."

"It won't. She's it for me," Liam admits, making my lower belly flutter to life.

Callum gives him a knowing nod. "I know, man, it's always been her."

Liam rubs at the back of his neck. "You knew?"

Callum laughs. "Of course I fucking knew. I think we all did, except for V, of course."

Liam's arm wraps around my waist and he pulls me to his side.

"Aww, look at you two. But please, as cool as I am with this, can we make an agreement to keep the public displays of affection to a minimum?"

Before I can even reply, Liam spins me in his arms and I brace myself to not collide with his chest.

"Sorry, man, I can't make any promises. I like knowing I can kiss V whenever I want."

And with that, he lowers his mouth to mine, making his intentions clear.

"And on that note…"

I hear the door clicking shut behind us and Liam pulls me to his hard body as he continues to devour my mouth. When we part, we're both a little breathless. He takes my hand without a word and tugs me with him until we return to my room.

Chapter Thirty-Nine

Liam

"Okay, we're going out today, so up and at 'em."

She rolls over, taking the duvet with her, grumbling into the pillow.

"Verity." I sneak my hand underneath the duvet until I come into contact with her silky-smooth skin, and as tempting as it would be to get back under there with her and give her a proper wakeup call, it will mean our entire day will be shot to hell, and I don't want to waste it. So, before I can get distracted, I begin tickling her, which has the desired effect as she shoots up and practically propels of the edge of the bed to get away from me.

"Liam, if you're trying to get on my good side, you're doing very badly." She gets to her feet and crosses her arms, but it's impossible to take her seriously when she's standing there with her hair a mess from a night of letting me worship her, and that tiny as sin T-shirt.

"It's not funny." She pouts.

I hold up my finger. "Okay, hold that thought." I move to go past her but make a point of giving her arse a little slap as I do, and I hear her huff out an ineligible curse. Grabbing the tray where I left it, I return, and her eyes roam to the tray then back to my face.

Her hand goes to her chest. "Liam Carmichael, did you get me Starbucks?"

"I did, now sit." I nod towards the bed, and she bites her bottom lip. If there's one thing I've noticed about Verity since we've been sleeping together, she loves it when I take charge, even if she does like to give me sass in return.

"Say the magic word first," she says playfully.

"Please, baby." Her lips part and she does as I ask.

I move to sit beside her and place the tray between us.

"Almond Croissant and a Caramel Macchiato, my lady," I say, handing her the coffee. She smiles and inhales a deep breath as she brings it to her nose before taking a small sip.

"Why thank you, kind sir, my favourites."

Picking up my own coffee, I smile behind the rim. "Keep that up and we might stay in and play out a little fantasy instead."

Her nipples grow hard under the material of her top and I push the tray aside and reach over, my hand going to her thigh, squeezing before trailing my fingers across her soft skin, loving how it pebbles with goosebumps from my touch, and then I roam until I'm at the apex of her thighs. She spreads her knees a fraction, and I can't help myself when I slowly slide my thumb through her slit.

"Oh God." She gasps, and I look up to find her eyes fixed on my hand, watching every move of my finger as I bring it close to her core.

"Do you like me touching you, V?"

Her eyes go straight to mine. "Always."

I can't hide my smirk as I push my middle finger between her folds and into her hot entrance.

"Fuck," she says, clenching around my finger.

But before I get lost in her, I pull my hand away, bring my

finger to my mouth, suck it, and then I release it with a soft wet sound.

"My favourite," I say, holding her gaze with mine.

Her mouth is agape, waiting to see what I'll do next, so I just bring my coffee to my lips and take a large sip, the burn welcome from denying myself.

I point to the croissant. "Come on, eat up and finish your coffee, we need to be out of here in the next half an hour."

"What?"

Leaning over, I give her a chaste kiss before getting to my feet.

"I'll go get ready and meet you downstairs," I say, not looking back as I exit her room and laugh all the way to Callum's when I hear her let out a frustrated moan.

Good, it will only make today that much more pleasurable when we do get back.

"Are you going to tell me where we're going?" she asks as we both pull on our masks before entering Camden tube station.

"Nope," I say, taking her hand in mine after we've both tapped in and go down the escalators to wait on the platform.

As soon as we get on the tube, we both take a seat, and she watches me, waiting for me to tell her what stop, but I pretend to be busy on my phone. And then I grab her hand and point to where she's sitting.

"Did you know there are four London landmarks hidden in the seat pattern?"

Verity shakes her head and looks at me, and then she moves aside to look at her seat.

"Really? It just looks like a jazzy, eighties-vibe pattern to me."

I shake my head and take her index finger and point.

"What do you see there?" She stares for a moment, and then her eyes dart back to mine.

"Big Ben."

"Yep, and what do you see there?" Moving her finger to the next one, she looks down again.

"Shit, is that St. Paul's Cathedral?"

Smiling, I'm not surprised she spotted it so fast.

"It is. There's two more though. Do you think you can find them?"

A minute goes past when her head shoots up.

"London Eye?"

Her eyebrows rise when she asks, and I nod, wishing we weren't wearing masks so I could lean in and kiss her.

"Yep, but can you find the last one?"

She squints as she searches the fabric, and I see her sigh rather than hear it over the sound of the tube.

I quickly lift her, pulling her into my lap, gaining a glare from the commuter opposite, but I don't give a shit.

Taking her hand, I point out one part and then trail her finger to the other.

"You see those?"

She nods.

"Those are the two columns of Tower Bridge."

"You're shitting me?" she says, just as the tube pulls up to a station, her voice coming out louder, and I can't help but laugh.

"I shit you not."

I move her back to her seat and I notice the commuter now checking out his seat between his legs.

"How do you even know that?" she asks, but before I can answer, a pregnant lady gets on wearing a badge and I jump to my feet and offer her my seat. Her eyes smile even though I can't see her mouth, and when I look at Verity, she gets to her feet and joins me by the door.

"We have another two stops," I say. "You don't have to stand yet."

She takes my hand in hers. "I want to stand with you, and besides, I now know we're getting off at Leicester Square."

I just nod, clearly giving myself away when I said how many stops we had to go.

"Very sneaky." I pull her to my body, thinking of all the times growing up how I wished I could do this—be with her like this.

"So, are you going to tell me how you knew that? I've been using the underground for years and I've never even noticed."

The platform is busy when we get off and I keep hold of her hand as we change over to the Piccadilly line, which is only like three hundred yards, and to be fair, we could just walk, but I want to keep her guessing.

As soon as we hop on the tube, I don't bother sitting and I lean on one on the padded seats at the back of the carriage and hold her against me before we get off at Covent Garden.

Chapter Forty

Verity

Liam never ceases to surprise me, and I love him sharing things with me that I wasn't aware of before. I mean, it's not that I haven't noticed how polite and courteous he is, he's always been that way, and maybe if I didn't already know him, I might think it were an act, but he's nothing like James in that regard.

As quickly as we're on the tube, we're stepping off again at Covent Garden.

I look at him and he just smiles, and again, he's brought me to one of my favourite places.

I love coming here and strolling through The Apple Market. It used to be the home to fruit and veg sellers, but now it's full of shops, restaurants, and daily markets. And I love everything about it—the sounds, the smells, the people.

We go towards the lift, but the queue is ridiculous.

I cock my head towards the stairs. "Shall we just take the stairs?"

He squeezes my hand. "You sure? It's one hundred and ninety-three steps."

I laugh and raise an eyebrow. "Yes, I am well aware it's the equivalent of fifteen floors, thank you very much."

Pulling on his hand, we move towards the spiral staircase.

"Anyone would think you're insinuating I'm too old or unfit to take the stairs," I chide.

His laugh fills me with warmth.

"Never," he says, close to the shell of my ear, sending sparks to all my nerve endings.

Truth is, one hundred and ninety-three steps might not be a lot to some people, but it is to others, and as we start walking, we see some who have to stop and take a breather. If it wasn't for the fact that I'm currently trying to prove a point, I'd be joining them.

When we get outside, the first thing I do is remove my mask and take a deep breath as I try to get control of my breathing.

Liam slips his mask off and pulls me close to his side and kisses my temple and tucks his hand in the back of my jean pocket—such an expected action but a pleasant one. He always makes me feel protected.

"Let's grab a drink and then hit the market," he suggests. I nod and notice how he looks around, scoping out the area and people, and I wonder if he's aware he's doing it, like he's slightly on guard.

"Are you okay?" I ask, pulling him to a stop.

He smiles, showing me his teeth. He has one bottom tooth that slightly overlaps. It's perfectly imperfect, and I love it.

I glance towards a small group of girls who are openly appraising him, and before I can stop myself, I go up onto tiptoes and give him a slow, deliberate kiss, claiming him as mine.

"What was that for?" he asks, his eyes shining.

"Just a thank you kiss."

He wiggles his eyebrows. "And to think today isn't even over yet. I look forward to the kiss you'll give me when we get home."

Why is it him referring to my parents' as home floods my lower belly with butterflies?

"Come on. Cocky much?" I tug on his hand.

Inside the market, we take our time as we go from stall to stall and into the shops. Everyone is pretty much keeping to social distancing, and there are hand sanitisers as far as the eyes can see.

We're looking at some prints from Photo Typewriter.

"If you like them, let me buy them for you," Liam says, pulling my back to his chest and leaning his masked covered chin on my shoulder.

I shake my head and step out of his arms.

"Come on, let's go," I say.

We move until we reach Forks for Jewellery. It's one of my favourites, and they have these candle holders made from spoons. James always mocked me about my tastes.

"I love these," I say, picking one up and having a look.

"You should get them for when you get your new place."

And that right there is the difference between them. He encourages me to get the things I like without judgement.

It's so hard to retrain my brain to not automatically go to James, even with something as simple as buying something for when I move, and even though it has fuck all to do with him.

I start speaking to the vendor when Liam points over his shoulder. "I'll be back in a minute," he says, and before I can respond, he disappears.

After purchasing two of the candlestick holders, I wait nearby and check my phone until Liam returns with a bag in his hand, but before I can be nosey, he wraps his arm over my shoulder.

"Okay, you ready for lunch?"

"Starving," I reply.

"Good, because I booked us a table."

Taking hold of my hand, we make our way back outside of the market. We stop to watch a street performer where Liam drops some money for them and then he leads the way, and when we turn the corner, I already know where he's taking me.

"Browns." He still has his mask on, but I know he's smiling when we enter, and he gives his name to the host who sees us to a round wooden table with two brown chairs.

Once we're seated, Liam picks up the menu and starts looking when a server comes over and takes our drinks order.

We both decide on a Wonderland Sour, seeing as neither of us has had it before, and he also asks for a bottle of still water.

"Well, what are you going to eat?" he asks me, when he lays down his menu and takes hold of my free hand.

"What are you having?"

"Mushrooms on sourdough for starters, steak frites main, and then apple and damson crumble for dessert."

I bite my lip. "Did you look up the options when you booked it?"

He holds up his hands. "Yeah, guilty."

Liam always took forever to choose when we'd go out to eat with my family and he'd come along with Callum.

"Well played. Fuck it, I'll have the same."

His eyes go wide, and I laugh. "Except for starters, I'll have the beetroot and goats cheese salad instead."

"Wow, for a minute there I thought you'd been swapped out with an alien."

Our drinks arrive and we order our food before Liam makes a toast.

"To many more days like today."

We clink glasses and then he hands over the bag.

"Liam." My cheeks heat and I wish I was wearing my

mask so I could hide the fact. Other than my family, I'm not used to being given something for no reason. When I peep inside, I see the prints I was looking at when we were at Photo Typewriter. "You didn't need to do that," I say, and then before I can talk myself out of it, I pass him the small box from the bag I have my candlestick holders in.

    I know how much he loves the ocean and when I saw this silver shell ring, I just got it on impulse. And I swear I feel sweat pooling in the middle of my shoulder blades as I pass him the small box, and now he's the one visibly blushing. It's not something I'm used to seeing.

Chapter Forty-One

Liam

"What's this?" I clear my throat and take the box from Verity as she looks down at the table.

"It was stupid. I saw it and thought of you, the vendor said I could return it if you didn't like it—"

Cutting her off, I take hold of her hand and squeeze, needing to reassure her. I'm sure whatever it is, I'll love it just because of the simple fact it's from her.

Opening the box, I blink as I stare at a silver shell, and when I remove it, I can see it's a ring made from a small teaspoon.

"Wow, this is… I love it." I look up and find her eyeing me suspiciously. "Verity, I love it, honestly."

I slide it onto my ring finger on my right hand. The fit is spot on and I hold it up to have a look.

"You promise you're not just saying that?"

Moving from my seat, I crouch down in front of her and rest my hands on her knees.

"No, V. I wouldn't lie to you." I reach up and stroke the crimson blush over her cheek and then pull her face to mine and give her a chaste kiss before returning to my seat, just in time for the arrival of our starter.

"Oh my God. I am so full." Verity puts her hand over her stomach, and I imagine her doing that with our baby inside her, the thought dropping out of nowhere. I mean, I barely imagined this... us, being together, but the thought of a future, a *real* future together hits me out of nowhere.

"Thank you, that was so good."

I reach under the table and squeeze her knee. "You're welcome."

"I'm just going to use the ladies' room," she says as she puts on her face mask.

Nodding, I sit back, and when the server comes back, I ask for the bill. Just as they come back and I'm paying, Verity returns and tilts her head to the side, raising her eyebrows, and I just shrug. Today was my idea, she just needs to suck it up.

"Next time, I'm paying," she says, pulling her jacket off the back of the chair and putting it on.

"Yes, love." I slip on my mask, and then together, we make our way out. We thank the server and the host, and I take her hand in mine just as we exit the door.

She stops suddenly and my shoulder bumps into her.

"Everything all right?" I ask and slide down my mask now we're outside.

"James," she says, her voice cracking.

Standing before us is her jerk of an ex.

"Verity," he says with a sly smirk as his eyes roam up and down her body before stopping at our joined hands. When she notices, she instantly lets go, and I grind my jaw.

"What's this?" he asks, waving between the two of us.

"None of your business," she says, but her voice is small. This is not the Verity I know and care about. "Come on." She goes to move past him, but his hand goes to her shoulder and instantly gets my back up.

"Take your hand off her now." My voice is deep and low as I try to hold back my anger at him even having the audacity to touch her.

He looks to me, then back to Verity, before he lets his hand fall away.

"Is this a joke? You're kidding, right? You and him? Your little brother's best friend, really?" I hear the gasp escape her lips.

"No, yes, it's none of your business," she says, and again her voice is trembling.

The dickhead throws his head back and laughs, and I clench my fists either side of me as I try not to let my emotions get the better of me. And this, coming from the guy who had the privilege of being with her and treated her like a fucking doormat, like she was beneath him.

"You really are scraping the barrel, aren't you? You've even put on weight."

Before I can stop myself, I lunge for him, gripping his T-shirt in my fists and pushing him backwards.

"Shut your fucking mouth. Do not talk to her. Do not even fucking look at her." He staggers back as I push him off the curb and into the road. He visibly swallows, his eyes wide.

He tries to shake me off but I'm livid, and the only colour I'm currently seeing is red.

"Shit, Liam, let him go, please, let's go." Verity's hand clasps my shoulder, and when I look back to her, I notice a small crowd is forming.

"What the fuck is going on, J?" says a guy as he comes to stand beside James and looks between us. I haven't seen him before, but from the way he looks at Verity with recognition, he must be his friend.

"Steve, it's just a misunderstanding," Verity says as she tugs on my hand.

I let go of his top but shove him as I do. He staggers again, but his friend steadies him.

Verity turns away and tugs me along with her.

"That's it, run off with your little fuck boy. He'll get bored soon enough, just like I did."

I don't stop to think as I round on him, and in less than three strides, I pull my arm back and punch him hard in the jaw, followed by a loud crack as he falls onto his arse. His mate looks at me and holds his hands up.

Someone shouts out something, but Verity is gripping the bottom of my top as she hurriedly tries to drag me down a side road.

"Fucking hell, Liam," she whisper-shouts, looking back the way we came. "You didn't need to hit him," she chastises.

I just raise an eyebrow. My adrenaline is pumping, and I'm wired. I know if I'm not careful and I open my mouth, it might come out wrong, and I won't be able to take it back.

"Seriously, you have nothing to say for yourself?" she asks, crossing her arms.

Shaking my head, I turn my back on her and start walking.

"Shit, Liam, wait." She's breathless as she tries to catch up with me. "Would you stop?"

I ignore her and keep moving until I can no longer hear the sound of her footsteps behind me.

"Please, Liam." Her plea causes my steps to falter.

I bow my head and wait until she's beside me. I take a deep breath in through my nose and out through my mouth.

"Liam, please would you talk to me?"

Raising my eyes, I meet hers as she moves to stand in front of me and then pulls me to the side, away from prying eyes.

"I'm not going to apologise for hitting him, he deserved way worse, and you know it." I hold up my hand and tick off my fingers. "Firstly, he touched you. Secondly, he insulted you. And thirdly, he fucking touched you."

I drop my hand and clench them both into fists. "But do you know what the real killer was?"

She shakes her head, worrying her lip, waiting for me to continue.

"When he looked down at us holding hands and you let go. You let go, V, and it fucking hurt. It hurt more than my fist connecting with his jaw. It hurt right here." I bring my hand to my chest and thump it, which causes her to flinch, and even though I would never hurt her, it still makes me feel like an arsehole. I can't do this, not here, not now.

Chapter Forty-Two

Verity

Fuck, I've never seen him so angry, or hurt for that matter, and it's all my fucking fault.

"Let's call it a day, V."

My heart is hammering in my chest as my pulse begins to beat erratically. "What? What do you mean?" I say, my voice panicked. He goes to step past me, but I block him and do the same when he moves to the opposite side.

He pinches his nose, and I can see his nostrils flaring as he squeezes his eyes closed before opening them and staring at me. Eyes that were sparkling with happiness not so long ago now look dull and void.

"Verity, I need a minute, okay? Let's just go home, please." His jaw clenches and I see he needs to cool off.

I wrap my arms around my middle and nod, stepping aside, and he starts walking. I follow closely behind, keeping my head cast down, feeling like all eyes are on me.

He glances back a few times to make sure I'm still with him, but otherwise he keeps facing forward. We bypass Covent Garden, which is exit only and head straight to Leicester Square, which is about six minutes away.

When we reach the station and the gates, he stops and

waves his arm for me to go first and follows close behind me. I feel the warmth of his hand on my lower back when we ride the escalator down, and again when we get on the tube, but other than that, he makes no other contact.

I take one of the seats and he stands, leaning on the padded seat, and he stares at his feet the whole time. It takes ten minutes to go six stops, but it feels a lot longer when we finally exit at Camden Town.

"Do you want to walk or take a cab?" he asks, his voice deep and thick as we exit the station.

I worry my lip and look around. "Cab if one is free. If not, might as well just walk," I reply.

He nods and says nothing else. There's a cab, so we're home within fifteen minutes.

As soon as we go through the front door, my dad smiles from the living room couch.

"Nice day, kids?"

"Yeah, it was nice," Liam says, moving to go past me. "Sorry, I need the little boys room." He takes the stairs two at a time and I let out a heavy breath.

My dad tilts his head in a silent question, but I just shake mine in response and go upstairs to my room. I pull my jacket off and throw it on the back of the chair and let out a groan as I sit on the edge of my bed, picking at my nail polish.

As soon as Liam enters and closes the door behind him, I'm on my feet.

"Please, Liam, will you talk to me?"

He swallows hard and I see the way his shoulders move up and down when he lets out a resigned sigh.

I desperately want to touch him, but I'm afraid if I do, he'll push me away, and I don't think my heart can take it.

"How would you have felt if we happened upon one of my exes and I let go of your hand?"

I open my mouth to reply and try to form a response, and after stuttering like a fool, I finally manage a reply.

"I'd be hurt. I'm sorry. But it has nothing to do with you and everything to do with me."

I watch as he grinds his jaw, hating how the most amazing day got ruined so fucking quickly.

"I was blindsided. Out of nowhere, he was just standing there in front of me, looking at me with disdain. I'm not ashamed to be with you, Liam."

He huffs out of his nose. "Is that why you stumbled over your words when he asked?"

I cross my arms. "That's not fair, and it's none of his business. I didn't want him tainting what we have, and he managed to do it anyway in less than a couple of minutes."

He shakes his head and leans against the wall, crossing his arms, the ring on his finger catching the light. He's hurting and it's my fault.

"Sorry, Liam, but I knew I'd fall off the pedestal you put me on sooner or later."

He shakes his head. "I don't have you on a pedestal."

I raise my eyebrows and he lets out a resigned sigh. "Fine, okay, I might have had you on a tiny stool, but you're worth so much more than his disrespect. And yeah, I might just be your little brother's best friend, but I would rain down hellfire on anyone, and I mean fucking anyone, who ever hurts you."

"I know and I'm sorry."

Unable to stop myself, I grip his forearms until he uncrosses his arms as I take his hand in mine, his knuckles already swelling as I bring it to my mouth.

"I hate that you're hurt because of me," I whisper and then kiss his hand softly.

His free arm wraps around my waist, pulling me closer to his body.

"I'm not hurt because of you. I'm hurt because he opened his mouth and I lost my temper. That's all on me, Verity. And for that, I apologise."

"You don't have to be sorry. I do. I'm not embarrassed to be with you. I was blindsided by him, that's all."

I go up on my tiptoes and wrap my arms around his neck.

"And for what it's worth, I'll never pull away from you again. And even though I don't normally condone violence, I'm secretly glad you punched him."

He laughs at that and dips his head until his mouth hovers over mine.

"Does that mean we're good?" he asks.

I smile, feeling like a weight has been lifted. "We're good," I reply.

"Good, because I'm so fucking in love with you, Verity Warren."

Before I have a chance to reciprocate my feelings, he kisses me with a fierce ferocity I've never felt before. Silently we kiss between removing our clothes as he lays me down on the bed, covering me with his body but keeping his weight off me. He studies my features as he slowly slides into me, and I wrap my legs around him, arching my back until he's balls deep.

And I know in this moment, it's not just sex or fucking like so many other times—times I refused to acknowledge Liam is making love to me. But this time, we're kindred as I make love to him too, and the final puzzle piece I've always been missing finally finds its place, and it's right here with Liam Carmichael.

Chapter Forty-Three

Verity

After we finish making love, Liam holds me close. Neither of us speaks as we let our hearts return to normal, but I'm beginning to think that's impossible when I'm with him like this. He squeezes me a little tighter, telling me without words he never wants to let me go, which is fine by me, as I'm right where I want to be. My leg is thrown over his thigh and I'm resting over his chest when he reaches for my hand and I notice the slight swelling.

"Do you want me to get you some ice?" I ask, kissing his knuckles.

"No, it's fine."

And then he takes my index finger, pointing to the ceiling. "You see those?"

I nod. "Yeah, the stars Callum put up when I was camping with the girl guides," I reply.

He holds me against him, and I feel rather than see him shake his head.

"No, they would be the stars *I* put up." It's hard to miss the affection in his voice. "Callum was too busy reading one of your teen magazines and getting a boner."

I try to pull my hand free to slap his chest, but he just laughs. "Liam, don't say shit like that."

He kisses the top of my head. "Fair enough, that was a bit too much information."

"You think?"

He ignores me and carries on. "Anyway, those stars, that was me." He starts to move my hand, my index finger straight like a wand under his.

"C.A.R.I.A.D." He makes the shape of each letter, saying each one out loud as he goes.

When he closes his hand gently over mine, I say the word. "Cariad." I tilt my head to look up at him and lick my lips. "But the locket was years later, that was when I was like twelve."

He nods, his eyes so incredibly vulnerable.

"Because it's only ever been you, V, always."

His words manage to shatter any remaining resolve I might have had left, and if I hadn't already fallen for him, this moment right here would have had me free falling.

Like he always does, he's baring his soul to me. "I love you, Verity Warren, and I will until the day I die, and thereafter."

My breath catches in my chest as I attempt to respond.

The pad of his thumb brushes over my bottom lip.

"It's okay, V. You don't have to say anything back, I know this is a lot. Besides, I can wait."

My heart squeezes. Liam is always waiting. I shake my head and pull his thumb away from my mouth.

"I get it, Verity, the last man you gave your heart to broke it."

I swallow the lump in my throat. "Yes and no, but the thing is, Liam, I do love you."

I held back those words, worried what they would mean, and I realise now it was selfish of me. He's shown me so many times how he cares about me, and I feel like I'll never be able to catch up and show him how much he makes me feel loved, cherished, and worshipped.

"What?" He blinks a few times, as if coming out of a haze. "Please don't fuck with my heart, Verity."

He says that in a pained voice, his hand squeezing mine in his as he sits up, taking me with him, and I place my other hand over his heart.

"I'm not, Liam. I would never say it if it wasn't true. I'm sorry I held it back for so long, but I do love you, Liam, very much so."

He cups my cheeks in both of his calloused palms and leans his forehead against mine as he takes a deep breath in through his nose and out through his mouth and then leans back, holding my face firmly in place.

"Then please say it one more time, so I know I'm not dreaming."

My lips curve up into a smile and I annunciate each word. "I. Love. You. Liam. Carmichael."

His mouth comes down on mine so fast I can barely catch my breath. His teeth knock against mine, the kiss is so desperate and unyielding, but I wouldn't change it for anything in the world.

When he pulls back, our breathing is ragged, and he rests his forehead on my shoulder. I feel him shake his head slightly, as if he still can't quite believe me.

Reaching out, it's now my turn to hold his face in my palms.

"I'm here, Liam, with you. This,"—I point between us—"it's real, and I love you."

His eyes glisten with so much emotion I have to swallow down the urge to cry.

"Do you know how many times I conjured this up in my mind? That my feelings for you would be reciprocated?"

Now I'm the one shaking my head. "I'm just sorry it took me so long to catch up. I feel like I wasted so much time, too blind to see what was standing right in front of me."

He places the pad of his thumb on my bottom lip. "No, you didn't, we both had growing to do, and it wasn't the right time. But this, right here, right now, this is our time, Verity. You and me."

"Yeah," I reply, blinking back tears.

"Abso-fucking-lutely it is."

I take a deep breath. "Well, okay, in that case, how would you feel about moving in with me?"

He looks stunned—even more surprised than when I said I loved him.

"Are you serious?"

"I am. We've already survived a lockdown together and it seems stupid you looking for somewhere when my place is almost ready, which can just as easily be our place."

Over two months I've pretty much spent every day with this man, and for once, I'm throwing caution to the wind and doing what I want.

"Our place." He rolls the words around in his mouth as though he's tasting them.

"So, is that a yes?"

If I was standing right now, then his smile alone would knock me off my feet.

"Yes."

I throw my arms around his neck.

"Shit, we're really doing this."

He pulls back. "We are, unless you're already having second thoughts?"

I shake my head. "Not at all. But you can be the one to tell Callum, and there'll be ground rules. He can't just come and go as he pleases." Not that rules would stop Callum, of course, they are best friends after all.

"Whatever you say, baby."

He lowers his mouth to the side of my throat. "I think we should celebrate," he whispers against my skin.

"Oh, you do, do you?"

Flicking out his tongue, he licks my neck. "Yep."

"And what did you have in mind?" I ask, breathless.

"How about I show you…"

Epilogue

TWO YEARS LATER

Liam

Things have been non-stop, with Verity leaving her job at her accounting firm to go full time with her small business and me working on my degree and website design part time, we barely have time to just be together. So, I made her take a mid-week break with me.

"Liam, where are we going?" she asks again, kicking her bare feet up on the dashboard.

I reach over and squeeze her thigh.

"Baby, if we have an accident, you'll lose all your teeth."

She drops her legs and squeezes my hand.

"Sorry, I just want to know where we're going."

I glance over and she pouts out her lower lip, and I can't help but laugh. She huffs and crosses her arms, looking out of her window.

"What the hell is in Stadhampton anyway?" she ponders out loud.

"You'll find out. Now do me a favour and put this on."

I reach down beside me and pull out the eye mask and pass it to her.

"Oh, do I have to?"

"Yes, we're almost there, just humour me." She slips on her shoes and then does as I ask.

Checking her eyes are covered, I wave my hand in front of her face. Satisfied, I continue driving, and after about five more minutes, I pull into the car park and switch off the engine.

"Okay, we're here."

Her hand moves to the mask, but I reach out and stop her.

"Easy, tiger." I bring her fingers to my lips and kiss them. "Let me come around and let you out, and promise no peeping."

She smiles. "I promise."

I unclip my seat belt and watch her as I get out and go around to her door, opening it. She's already following her seatbelt until she finds the buckle and releases it.

"Okay, you can take it off," I say, crouching down.

Removing it, she blinks a few times and then runs her fingers through her hair.

I hold out my hand for her.

"Me lady."

She laughs and takes mine in hers as she climbs out of the car and looks around.

Her eyes stop when she sees the two large wooden carved bears either side of a foliage covered arch leading to a converted London route master bus, with a neon sign that reads 'reception'.

I pull her to my side. "Do you remember when you and Maxine went for afternoon tea at Crazy Bear in Beaconsfield?"

She tilts her head to look up at me, a big grin adorning her face when it registers where we are.

"Well, I booked us a suite here at their original venue."

"Oh my God, this is amazing."

I laugh. "We haven't even checked in yet."

"Are you serious? I can't believe you did this. Liam Carmichael, have I told you lately how much I love you?"

Grabbing her arse, I squeeze. "Maybe once or twice when I woke you up with my tongue in your pussy."

She swats my chest, her entire face glowing red, and I lean down and take her in a not so chaste kiss. Forcing myself to pull back, I go around to the boot of the car and grab her travel case and my travel bag and swing it over my shoulder.

She grabs her handbag from the footwell and we lock up the car.

We check in and are both given a glass of champagne as we're taken in a golf cart to the deluxe suite located in one of the renovated cottages surrounding the converted pub. Every room and suite are different and individually designed.

Our suite is decked out floor-to-ceiling in various tones of gold, and at the foot of the double bed is a roll top copper bath.

Verity walks over to the bed and strokes the gold velour textured throw and cushions before spinning in a slow circle and looking up to the ceiling and then back again as she takes in the room. I already knew that even though it's a suite, the rooms are not particularly large, and I pre-booked the biggest one they had, but the eccentric style more than makes up for it. I hold my breath as I wait for her reaction.

"Oh my God. Liam, this is amazing."

I let out a relieved breath, wrap her in my arms and rest my chin on her shoulder.

"Happy anniversary, baby."

She tilts her face to the side to look at me. "What?"

I smile and kiss the tip of her nose. "It's two years since you walked in on me in your parents' living room."

"You are such a romantic."

"Believe me, you haven't seen anything yet."

She brings her champagne up to her lips and takes a sip before turning to face me.

"Please tell me we're going to be trying out that bath later."

"We can do anything you want to. I thought we could go check out the farm, stretch our legs after the drive, and then come back and relax for a bit and get ready for dinner. I hope you don't mind, I booked us reservations at the Thai restaurant."

"Of course I don't mind. I just can't believe how lucky I am."

I shake my head. "No, V, I'm the lucky one."

Verity

I never would have guessed this was where he was bringing us for a mid-week getaway. I still can't get over it. If I thought the one at Beaconsfield was amazing, then this is phenomenal. It's flamboyant and eccentrically luxurious, if that's even a thing. There are wooden carved statues dotted about the garden and the myriad of decorative touches throughout adds style and character. A touch of class and madness in equal measures, not your typical beige hotel experience, that's for sure. Liam even went as far as to book us both a Thai couple's massage tomorrow too.

It even boasts its own farm. I didn't expect to come away

and see llamas, reindeers, pygmy goats, cattle, chickens, and sheep. I insisted we go back to the farm shop before we leave, there is no way I'm not taking back fresh farm produce when we go.

He left me a little something in the bathroom for me to wear tonight—my favourite bullet massager. I love knowing he has the control at his fingertips, and the thought alone sends a thrill of excitement through me. I love experiencing these things and I wouldn't want to do that with anyone else.

Liam stayed out of the way while I got dressed, and I'm so glad I packed my little black dress, and from the way he swallows and adjusts himself, I'd say he is too.

"Fucking stunning."

He circles his finger for me to turn, and I do, taking my time until I'm facing him again.

"You look handsome," I say as he comes over.

"Damn it, I want to kiss you so bad." His eyes are dark and full of all the bad things I hope he's going to do to me later.

"It's okay, I have my super stay lipstick, kiss away."

He groans.

"Why is that a bad thing?" I question.

"I won't lie, I love it when you suck my dick and your lipstick smears all over me and your mouth."

"Oh, my bad, I'm sorry."

Before I can pull away, his lips are on mine, and I buck as a vibration rolls through me.

"Fuck," I say, pulling out of the kiss. He gives me a wicked smile and turns it off.

"Later. Until then, expect more of where that came from."

He wasn't joking when he said I could expect more of where that came from. I was just grateful we had our dinner alfresco and outside—it felt more private, thank God, but no less intense. I swear, he'll be the death of me. I never knew how much of a thrill this kind of thing was, and if anything, it'll only make him all the more wild when we finally get back to the bedroom. That's if he can wait that long.

"You're insatiable," I say, slightly breathless. I swear he kept bringing me to the brink so many times, but this time, he let me come, I know he did. He knows when I'm about to fall over the edge. I take another sip of champagne, the bubbles tickling my nose.

"Only for you. Here." He pulls out the pouch from his pocket and places it in my hand as he leans over, capturing my lips with his mouth before I take myself to the bathroom. I can't help but appreciate how beautiful the gardens are all lit up like this, it's amazing.

When I return, he's bouncing his leg up and down, wiping his palms on his thighs.

"Hey, you okay?"

He startles and laughs when I move back to my seat.

"Yeah, fine. I've settled the bill. You ready to go back to our suite?"

I nod and he reaches for my little trench coat and helps me into it when I stand up.

We take the gold cart back to our suite, and like the gentleman he is, he comes around to my side and holds out his hand to help me out.

He opens our door and ushers me in first, and I kick off my shoes and undo my coat, leaving it on the arm of one of the high-back covered chairs beside our bed, and when I turn around, I notice all the rose petals sprinkled all over the bed, along with a single red rose and a note.

I look back to him and then reach for the note.

"Wow, when did you do this?" I ask, pulling the card out

from the tiny envelope. On one side is the word 'cariad' and the other a handwritten message from Liam.

Please say yes...

I look up and Liam is on one knee, holding open a small jewellery box. I cover my mouth, my hand shaking.

"Verity, to me you are beautiful in every way imaginable, inside and out. But your body is just the vessel that carries your soul, and that's the most beautiful thing about you. And we are nothing without our souls. Yours is the other part of mine, and without you, I am nothing. So, I'm asking you, Verity Warren, will you marry me? Please say yes..."

I step closer, afraid if I make any sudden movement I'll wake up and this will all be a dream—or I just overindulged in bubbly.

"Are you serious?" I ask, my voice scratchy.

He nods. "Yes, V. I love you more with each passing day. I feel selfish and greedy for loving you the way I do. Forever will never be enough. Marry me?"

I drop to my knees in front of him and reach out to hold his face in my hands.

"This is real... you want to marry me?"

He laughs. "Yes, my heart is and always will be irrevocably yours."

"Yes, yes, of course I'll marry you."

He smiles, drops to his other knee and leans in, meeting me for a slow, tender kiss.

"Thank you," he says, pulling back and holding up the box. I peer inside and gasp. The low light of the room does nothing to diminish how stunning the ring is. A platinum pear shaped halo engagement ring, diamond studded band. It's extravagant and elegant, exactly what I would have chosen for myself.

"It's beyond perfect, Liam." I sniff back tears.

He pulls it free and reaches for my shaking hand, but before he slides it onto my finger, he shows me the inside of the band. Engraved with one word is 'cariad'. I'm crying now, as he pushes it onto my ring finger. I hold up my hand and admire how breath-taking it is.

He takes my face in his hands and wipes the pads of his thumbs under my eyes.

"Thank you, Liam."

Smiling, he kisses me again. My entire body is alive and pumping with unspent adrenaline.

"I love you," I whisper when he draws back and rests his forehead against mine as we both try to get our breathing under control. He stands up and holds out his hand, gently guiding me to my feet.

"I love you too. Now hurry up and let your family know so I can spend the rest of the night making love to my fiancée," he says, patting my arse softly.

I laugh and shake my head. "No, Liam, they can wait until tomorrow. I just want this to be about you and me."

He scoops me up bridal style and walks over to the bed and drops me down, and I let out a laugh as he hovers over me.

"Now that I can get behind."

I wiggle my eyebrows at the double innuendo. "Oh, really?"

"Yes, really." His eyes are dark with desire, and my lower belly flutters with anticipation. "I plan on making my fiancée cum in every position, on every surface of this suite," he says as he unzips his trousers, and I reach up and start unbuttoning his shirt.

I don't know what I did to deserve this man, but I vow to make sure that no matter what we never go to sleep on an argument, and for him to know every day just how much I love him.

Acknowledgments

Always first and foremost, Mum, thank you for being the best mum, friend and house mate anyone could ever ask for and your unwavering support. Love you.

To my proofreader Crystal and my editor Lindsey, thank you.

My TiC's, Cassie, Crystal, Dusti and Julie, thank you for your love and endless support.

Amber, Ruth, Kayleigh, Kirsten & Layne, empowered women, empower women and I will never not be grateful to each and every one of you.

To my ARC readers, thank you so much for your continued support, I appreciate you all so much.

Author friends who support without motive or agenda, I see you. Community over competition, always.

Friends who are family, Grace, Dave & Tam. Victoria, William & Benjamin. Laura, Andy, Evie, Zach, & our mountain goat, Ethel.

Carlie my skin n blister, love you.

My family, I love you to the moon and back.

Jon, did you see my announcement? Miss you forever and a day.

Harley, my most loyal companion, gone but never forgotten.

About the Author

L.S. Pullen, aka Leila, was born and raised in North London, but now resides in Peterborough, England.

When she's not writing you'll find her walking her adopted pooch Luna. And taking care of her bunnies Bucky & Beatrix. She is passionate about everything books, lover of photography and art. And in true English cliche fashion, loves afternoon tea.

No longer working the corporate life, she's currently writing full time and managing a small business Cosy Book Stop and offers formatting services via Indie Author's Book Services.

- facebook.com/lspullenauthor
- instagram.com/lspauthor
- tiktok.com/@lspullenauthor
- bookbub.com/authors/l-s-pullen

Also by L.S. Pullen

Hearts of War

Where the Heart Is

Dysfunctional Hearts

Burning Embers

Midnight Embers

Forever Embers

Unforeseen Love

Unpredicted Love

Unexpected Love

Anthology:

Bluebonnet: A Romance Anthology for Uvalde

Coming Soon

Cruel Embers, Book 4 Coming Soon

Enchanted Embers, Book 5 Christmas Special Pre-Order Now

Printed in Great Britain
by Amazon